"I Never Thought You Would Turn Into A Smug, Stuck-Up Snob."

"Why don't you speak a little louder? I don't think they heard you over at table ten," Rafe quipped.

"Why do you care what they think? What does it matter to you if I lose my job?"

"Sarah, perhaps we should talk this out somewhere more private."

"Oh, so now you want to speak to me? After five months of ignoring my existence? After fourteen years of not even a postcard when you left for L.A. after graduation? I'm so sorry if hearing the truth makes you uncomfortable."

He'd opened his mouth to take her down a peg.... Then the absurdity of it all hit him. He was renowned for making top corporate raiders quake in their Gucci loafers, but fearless Sarah took him on without a wince.

Dear Reader,

How many people wish they could have a do-over in life? Well, that's exactly what Sarah Richards gets when her high school sweetheart, Rafe Cameron, returns to town. However, he's not quite the small-town boy she remembered now that he's built his financial empire, and she's no longer the naive girl next door.

In completing a book, I'm always nostalgic over saying goodbye to the characters. But Rafe and Sarah have an extra-special place in my heart since I had the privilege of chronicling their high school romance through short stories at the end of each of the five prior books in The Takeover series. Rafe and Sarah have worked hard and waited long for their happily ever after. I hope you enjoy reading how Rafe finally claims his small-town bride!

Happy reading!

Catherine Mann
www.CatherineMann.com

CATHERINE MANN

ACQUIRED: THE CEO'S SMALL-TOWN BRIDE

Special thanks and acknowledgment to Catherine Mann
for her contribution to The Takeover miniseries.

ISBN-13: 978-0-373-73103-9

Recycling programs
for this product may
not exist in your area.

ACQUIRED: THE CEO'S SMALL-TOWN BRIDE

Copyright © 2011 by Harlequin Books S.A.

This edition published by arrangement with Harlequin Books S.A.

For questions and comments about the quality of this book please contact us
at Customer_eCare@Harlequin.ca.

® and TM are trademarks of Harlequin Books S.A., used under license.
Trademarks indicated with ® are registered in the United States Patent
and Trademark Office, the Canadian Trade Marks Office and in other
countries.

www.Harlequin.com

Printed in U.S.A.

CATHERINE MANN

USA TODAY bestselling author Catherine Mann is living out her own fairy-tale ending on a sunny Florida beach with her Prince Charming husband and their four children. With more than thirty-five books in print in more than twenty countries, she has also celebrated wins for both a RITA® Award and a Booksellers' Best Award. Catherine enjoys chatting with readers online—thanks to the wonders of the wireless internet, which allows her to network with her laptop by the water! To learn more about her work, visit her website, www.catherinemann.com, or reach her by snail mail at P.O. Box 6065, Navarre, FL 32566.

To my sister Julie and her husband Todd—
high school sweethearts who are still celebrating
their happily-ever-after more than twenty years later!

* * *

Don't miss a single book in this series!

The Takeover
For better, for worse. For business, for pleasure.
These tycoons have vowed to have it all!

Claimed: The Pregnant Heiress by Day Leclaire
Seduced: The Unexpected Virgin by Emily McKay
Revealed: His Secret Child by Sandra Hyatt
Bought: His Temporary Fiancée by Yvonne Lindsay
Exposed: Her Undercover Millionaire by Michelle Celmer
Acquired: The CEO's Small-Town Bride by Catherine Mann

One

A veteran waitress at the Vista del Mar Beach and Tennis Club, Sarah Richards knew the number one rule for servers: never spill hot coffee on a man's *cojones*.

For the first time in fourteen years, she was tempted to risk her job.

Sarah tucked a signed receipt into the register while her gaze tracked along the lunch crowd to a table by the window. Where *he* sat. Her old high school boyfriend.

Rafe Cameron.

He settled into a chair across from his stepbrother, Chase Larson, seemingly oblivious to everyone else whispering about him even five months after his fateful homecoming. Why couldn't he have turned into a troll? Instead, the years had been so very kind to him. He looked even better than when they'd dated during their senior year. And he'd been mighty fine, unforgettable eye candy even then.

Rafe's blond hair had darkened to more of a tawny shade, his blue eyes icy-sharp even across the bustling dining room. Thick muscles roped his frame with a maturity that had only been hinted at during their teenage years when she'd wrapped herself around him in the back of his El Camino. Her traitorous body turned warm and tingly now, as it had then.

Apparently she hadn't made as large an impact on him. In all the time since he'd come back, Rafe Cameron hadn't spoken to her even once. At some point the man could have at least stuck out his hand for a "Hi, great to see you again" kind of greeting. She might have thought he was going so far as to avoid her. But it appeared she had become an insignificant part of his past.

The self-absorbed jackass deserved a pot of coffee in his lap.

Even worse than thumbing his nose at her, he'd stomped on the dreams of everyone in Vista del Mar. When the hometown poor boy returned as a mogul, everyone had hoped he would save the microchip factory, the small California community's lifeblood. But no. Last month, the *Seaside Gazette* had run an article announcing Rafe's plans to halt operations at the plant.

Just thinking about that exposé in the newspaper… Anger steamed to life hard and fast at the prospect of her hardworking parents losing their jobs. She slammed the register drawer with extra oomph. And in seconds she would speak to Rafe "Judas" Cameron since bad luck had placed him at one of her tables.

Eyes off the coffee, sister.

She needed this job. She didn't have a family trust fund cushion like the patrons dining here.

A quietly cleared throat interrupted her thoughts. Heaven forbid somebody would catch her gawking at Rafe and mistake her curiosity for rekindled interest. Expecting her boss or another waitress, Sarah spun around to find her grandmother, arms crossed and brows high.

Busted. Nobody got jack past Kathleen Richards. Best to play this cool though.

Sarah met green eyes the same shade as her own. Looking at Grandma Kat was like peering into a fast-forward mirror of herself a few decades from now, with the help of a little auburn hair dye. They even shared fiery natures, impulsive to the end. Although Kathleen edged closer to the flamboyant side as years went by. Sarah adored her, this woman who'd known the secret wishes of a preschooler that wanted roller skates rather than a china doll.

"Hi, Grandma Kat. Are you here for lunch?" She sidestepped a waitress balancing a tray. The scent of chlorine wafted in through the open French doors where some patrons ate lunch outside under sleek black umbrellas.

Kathleen had come to the exclusive club often during her tenure as personal assistant to Ronald Worth, prior owner of the microchip factory. "I think not. It's more than a little out of my price range now that I'm retired on a fixed income." She patted her purse, shaped like a pink-and-black bustier. "I've come to see you, sweetie, since you're ignoring my calls.

Nilda and I are meeting up at Bistro by the Sea. We would love for you to join us."

"So you can tell me all about whatever new eligible bachelor has crossed your path, a bachelor I absolutely must meet?" She winced at the possibility Grandma Kat may have caught her gobbling up Rafe with her eyes. "Seriously, have you ever considered opening a speed dating service?"

"You could be my first client." Her outrageous grandmother winked, silver Siamese cat earrings swaying.

Kathleen had doubled down on her matchmaking efforts last month once Sarah reached the third anniversary of her husband's death in a car accident. She missed Quentin, always would, but she would deal with that on her own, without well-meaning interference.

"Thanks, but I think I'll pass." Sarah hooked an arm around Kathleen for a quick hug, urging her toward the door flanked by palm trees. "Love you so much. Don't need the help. Now shoo. I have to work."

Best to take Rafe's order quickly, like bolting back bad-tasting medicine. A sense of dread swept through her at the thought of going over there. Not just because of her temper, but because of that traitorous heat he inspired with memories that clearly meant nothing to him, yet still had the power to make her heart beat faster.

Grandma Kat stayed stubbornly in her path. "Is there anything wrong with wanting to invite my favorite granddaughter out for coffee on her break?"

"I'm your *only* granddaughter and my break isn't for another hour. Stop worrying. I'm fine." Fine, and trying not to think about all the sensual reminiscences tied up with that infuriating man across the room. "I'm just concerned about the factory closing like everyone else."

Rafe's need for revenge against one person would cost the town so much—too much. During their teens, she'd listened to him plan how he would bring down Worth Industries, bring down Ronald Worth. When Rafe had left the night of graduation, she'd never expected him to carry those plans out, and especially not at the expense of so many others. It seemed like only yesterday they'd disdained the sort of people who threw away their hard-earned money on a single meal that cost more than some weekly grocery bills.

Kathleen gave Sarah's ponytail a teasing tug. "All right then. I'll let you off the hook—for now. But I really do need to speak with you. Let's have dinner tomorrow. I'll cook, and I already know that's your day off so don't try to fool me," her grandmother ordered, then fast-footed it out the door before Sarah could argue.

No more delays in speaking to Rafe. She checked his table, and sure enough, he hadn't done them all a huge favor by evaporating into thin air. And he still looked bad-boy dreamy, blond and rugged.

Her fist clenched around the pen and pad in her apron pocket, arming herself for the showdown. She strode across the dining room, toward the picture window with its million-dollar view of the Pacific. About fifteen feet above sea level, the club sported stone steps carved into the bluff leading to a sandy beach swept clean of pebbles. A natural cove, rocky and secluded and romantic—she knew that firsthand from when she'd dated Rafe.

As she closed the distance between them, snippets of conversation hit her ears like someone changing radio stations. A business deal was made over Cobb salads. At another linen-covered table, two wafer-thin trophy wives pushed fruit and cottage cheese around their plates while discussing jaunts to Hawaii.

Eyes on the target, she reminded herself.

Having him walk away after high school, never contacting her, had been painful. The way he acted now just made her plain old mad. She whipped out her pen and notepad with a speed worthy of any quick draw from a Wild West cowboy.

Waiting and wondering what it would be like to run into Rafe Cameron again had come to an end. She would take the lead in instigating a showdown reunion he would never forget.

Rafe Cameron had tried to forget Sarah Richards over the past fourteen years, with little success. The woman had stayed stamped in his memory long after she'd married some other guy mere seconds after Rafe left town.

Not that he held grudges. Much.

Half listening to his stepbrother seated across from him, Rafe watched Sarah make her way toward them. Red hair scraped back in a ponytail, she dodged a silver serving cart of tea and coffee. Her curvy body was mouthwateringly showcased in a simple white shirt with black slacks, typical uniform for the staff. But Sarah had always been anything but typical.

As she charged closer, her feisty temper crackled in her jade eyes. He was used to animosity since he'd announced his plans to close the factory. In fact, he was surprised Sarah hadn't unloaded on him sooner. She'd never been one to hold back in the past and she was gunning for bear now. Apparently some things never changed.

Like how his body reacted to just a simple glimpse of her heart-shaped face…her generous breasts. Heat pumped through him, uninvited and unwelcomed. He'd come back to Vista del Mar to settle a score, to destroy Worth Industries. After all, Ronald Worth had shown no mercy when firing Rafe's parents without cause. Rafe refused to feel guilty for doling out justice in his dead mother's name.

No one, not even Sarah Richards, would distract him.

She stopped at his table, pad and pen in hand. "May I take your order, Mr. Cameron?"

"Of course, Miss Richards." He spun the stem of his empty crystal glass between two fingers. "Or wait, that should be Mrs. Dobbs."

"It's Richards again."

A tic started in the corner of his eye. Interesting that she would return to her maiden name after Quentin Dobbs's death. "Sarah Richards then."

"Uh," his stepbrother, Chase Larson, interjected, looking from one to the other, "good to see you again, Sarah, but if you two will excuse me for a minute, I have to make a call. Just put me down for the pasta primavera and iced tea." With a half smile, Chase checked out.

Leaving Rafe alone with her.

He nudged aside his crystal glass. "Good to see you again, Sarah."

"*Oh*, so you do remember me." Acrimony dripped from her every word. "Not that you've so much as said boo to me since coming to town five months ago. That leads me to wonder. Are you too good to speak with your old friends these days?"

Surprise jolted him. How odd that she was mad about a rebuff, rather than the factory. Or at least that she'd found the slight important enough to bring up.

A flash of pride shot through him to register that far up on her radar after all this time. "That's a lot of animosity to carry around for a high school sweetheart."

"This isn't about the past." She jabbed the table with her pen. "It's about the present, how you're acting now. I'm surprised you have the guts to come here and casually knock back some cocktails after what you've done."

"It's lunchtime. Everybody's gotta eat, Kitten."

Her mouth went tight as he used his nickname from their past. They'd told the world his nickname for her had come because she looked so much like her grandmother—little kitten to Grandma Kat. But in reality, he'd given Sarah the label because of her temper—and because she'd left scratch marks on his back during a make-out session. And of course there was also that sweet way she purred in the back of her throat when he...

Rafe adjusted his tie. While they'd never gone all the way, they'd experimented plenty with other means for taking the edge off their sexual frustration. His thumb rubbed absently against two fingers and he could swear he still felt the silky slickness from bringing Sarah to completion.

Nostrils flaring, he tapped her notepad. "What's the lunch special today?"

"You're really going to pretend nothing's wrong? I guess I shouldn't be surprised. From what I hear you're so heartless now, you eat puppies and babies for breakfast." Her voice rose with each word, until two ladies in tennis skirts peered at her over their menus. "The way you're shutting down the plant, you're lucky nobody's poisoned your meals. Yet."

"Guess I'll have to hire a food taster." He'd forgotten about her sharp tongue, but rather enjoyed it now. Not many stood up to him these days. Most folks were too busy kissing his ass in hopes of currying favor.

Too fast, his mind zipped back to other ways she used to drive him crazy with that very same smart mouth of hers.

"It shouldn't be too tough to find a sucker willing to work for you since over half the town will be out of a job soon, thanks to you. Hey…" She snapped her fingers, her smile theatrically bright. "Maybe you have an application handy so I can pass it along to my parents since they'll undoubtedly be first to get the ax."

She had a lot of nerve chewing him out. He'd worked his tail off making something of himself after leaving this place. Every step of the way he'd envisioned riding back into town on his proverbial white horse and freeing Sarah from poverty's grip. Great plan. Except she'd quickly shifted her undying love to another guy, a man she'd married. Sure, the guy had died three years ago, but that didn't change the past.

So yeah, he'd ignored her since returning to Vista del Mar. Why the hell would he think she even wanted to speak to him now?

Gasping for air, Sarah paused her tirade, but not for long. "What? Nothing to say for yourself? You may have fooled some people at first with all your phony philanthropy, setting up a literacy charity in your mother's name. *Hannah's Hope*." She shook her head. "But you didn't trick me with your tax write-off attempt to get people to lower their guards. Is your need for revenge against Ronald Worth and his cronies really important enough to destroy so many lives?"

He held his peace for the moment, surprised— stunned even—to be called on the carpet so openly, so publicly. Although frankly, most of her accusations were true. He had come back to town for revenge. He was about to shut the factory and make a huge windfall.

Sure, the factory could be viable, but the effort and expense… No. He hadn't come this far in the work world by being a sap. And hell, yes, he was enjoying rubbing Ronald Worth's nose in every bit of the success.

But Sarah missed the mark in a huge and unforgivable way when she mocked anything to do with his mother. Anger steamed slowly. "Business is business, Kitten."

"Do *not* call me that." Her knuckles went white as she clenched her pen tighter.

Her ire fueled his own. "But that name holds such fond memories for me. Remember the way you—"

"Argh!" She stomped her foot. "I never thought you would turn into a smug, stuck-up snob."

"Why don't you speak a little louder? I don't think they heard you over at table ten."

"Why do you care what they think? What does it matter to you if I lose my job?" She plowed ahead with her rant, until the two women at the next table gave up all pretense of studying the menu and listened openly. "Do you even remember what it's like to work for minimum wage? To live paycheck to paycheck, all the time knowing you could lose your car or worse if a case of the flu keeps you out of work for a week?"

Conversations dwindled to a stop around the club. Not even a tink of silverware sounded, only muffled clanks from the kitchen.

"Sarah, perhaps we should talk this out somewhere more private."

"Oh, so now you want to speak to me? After five months of ignoring my existence? After fourteen *years* of not even a postcard when you left for L.A. after graduation? Well, screw you. I'm so sorry if hearing the truth makes you uncomfortable."

He'd opened his mouth to take her down a peg... then the absurdity of it all hit him. He was renowned for making top corporate raiders quake in their Gucci loafers, but fearless Sarah took him on without a wince.

A laugh rumbled low in his chest, rising and rolling out to fill the exclusive dining room.

"Damn it, Rafe, don't you dare laugh at me." Her face turned redder.

And he laughed harder.

A man with a "manager" pin on his jacket and harried look on his face wove his way around a table toward them. "Is there some kind of problem here, Mr. Cameron?"

"Not at all," Rafe said, trying his best to tamp down the laughter if not the urge to smile. "Ms. Richards and I were just catching up."

The manager turned to Sarah. "Ms. Richards, please do your 'catching up' on your own time."

"Of course. I'll be sure to keep my voice down, sir," she said tightly before facing Rafe again. "My apologies for popping your eardrums. Could I start you off with something to drink?"

She looked about as sorry as a kid caught with her hand in the cookie jar—after she'd eaten her fill.

"No apologies needed," Rafe answered, and couldn't resist adding, "Kitten."

Her eyes narrowed. Her chest heaved with a deep inhale, bringing to mind prom night when he'd seen her gorgeous breasts in the moonlight. They'd been in the back of his beat-up El Camino, under the stars, making out by the ocean. There hadn't been enough money to attend the after-party with their friends. He'd felt like crap for shortchanging her. But she'd sworn she didn't mind.

The next thing he knew, she'd skimmed aside the spaghetti straps on her gown and bared her breasts. He could still remember the smell of her wrist corsage, the feel of how she'd dug her kitten claws into his back with a sweet sigh.

Then he'd learned she was drunk because someone had spiked the punch. Their evening ended abruptly and he'd driven her to his house for sobering coffee.

Rafe skimmed a finger along his shirt collar. "Um, I'll take you up on that drink offer while I wait for Chase to finish his call."

Sarah smiled full out and with his brain too fogged with memories of her tight nipples against his chest he didn't bother analyzing what had made her grin.

She gestured to the silver drink cart a few feet away. "Some iced tea…or coffee perhaps?"

"Tea, thanks." He didn't need any more heat coursing through his body right now.

"Coming up in a jiffy." A gleam in her eyes, she hefted the cut-crystal pitcher full of amber and ice.

He picked up his empty glass and held it out for her. "Thanks."

"My pleasure."

The sparks in her jade eyes gave him a scant second's warning that she wasn't done with him yet. He should have remembered that Sarah didn't back down. He should have shaken off the mind-numbing memory of seeing her half-naked. Green eyes jewel-tone hard, she upended the pitcher….

And poured iced tea squarely onto his lap.

Two

Rafe jerked back in shock as Sarah dumped the pitcher full of iced tea over his lap. He dodged most of the contents, his chair clattering back against the floor. All the same, a hefty splash caught his legs, leaving his Brioni suit pants cold and clammy against his skin.

Sarah had always delivered the unexpected, something that apparently hadn't changed in fourteen years. Not many dared stand up to him these days and he had to confess he found the challenge refreshing. Chuckling softly, he swept beads of liquid from his thighs.

Around the room, silverware clattered against plates and chairs scraped back as curious diners zeroed in on them. Not that Rafe had ever cared what anyone else thought.

The manager charged toward him, face red. Rafe held up a hand stopping him in his tracks, then waving him away. He didn't have to bother checking to see if the manager honored his request. No one argued with him anymore.

Except Sarah.

Right now his entire focus stayed on the female in front of him, the one woman he could never forget. Fourteen years ago, she'd been a great big risk to his ambitions.

And now? Apparently he was every bit as drawn to her as ever. He laughed—at himself this time, because staying away from Sarah hadn't done him a damn bit of good.

Sarah slammed down the pitcher, anger steaming off her. "You think this is funny?"

Standing, he dipped his head close to her ear, close enough to catch a whiff of her floral shampoo. "I think I got under your skin."

Awareness crackled and the bustle of the dining room faded away. Her breasts swelled with each rapidly increasing breath. If he stepped so much as an inch closer, their bodies would brush, tempt, ignite. Her pupils widened with arousal, pushing through the sparkling green. Once he'd dreamed of draping her in emeralds to accent her eyes and making love to her naked other than the jewels. As a man who prided himself on reaching every goal he set for himself, leaving loose ends grated. But there wasn't going to be a positive outcome with Sarah. Only frustration piled on top of more frustration.

This was the very reason he'd stayed away from the Tennis Club and away from Sarah. He didn't need the distraction of an unresolved attraction dogging him, especially not now when he was so close to finally having his revenge on Ronald Worth.

Hauling his eyes off her, he snagged his suit coat from the back of his chair. "I'll need a to-go box for my lunch. How about you just have them pack up the daily special for both Chase and me? I'm not picky, but I am now in a hurry."

"Happy to accommodate that request." She smiled tightly.

"And put a lid on my tea," he couldn't resist taunting. "You'll have to pardon me if I'm suspicious of open containers around you."

"You're lucky I didn't pick the coffee," she said softly between gritted teeth.

He blinked back his surprise at the level of her anger, all because he hadn't been able to leave well enough alone. Including that one last urge to call her Kitten. Apparently that had crossed a line for her. While he knew she still stirred up a helluva fire in him, seeing that he ignited such a strong reaction in her as well gave him pause.

A hand on his shoulder startled him. He glanced back to see his stepbrother. Chase Larson didn't even bother hiding his surprise about the whole tea-soaked situation.

Anger faded from Sarah and a pink blush stole up her face as if she'd only just realized the magnitude of the scene she'd caused. Without a word, she spun away, sidling past the wary manager. She whipped her apron off and thrust her way through the double doors leading to the kitchen.

"Chase," Rafe said, pulling his eyes from the swinging doors and back to his stepbrother, "we're going to have to put the rest of our luncheon meeting on hold. As you can see, I need to change clothes."

Chase Larson was not only his stepbrother, but also handled Rafe's personal finances and some of his business dealings. They'd become stepbrothers when Rafe's dad married Chase's mom fourteen years ago. They hadn't spent any time living in the same house, but they shared a healthy rivalry that had helped propel them both out of poverty.

His stepbrother pulled his suit jacket from the back of the chair and shrugged it on again. "What the hell happened to you? Did you drop your drink or what?"

"Something like that." His eyes gravitated to the kitchen doors again where Sarah had disappeared seconds earlier.

He wasn't normally a man who wasted time on regrets, instead opting to charge forward and tackle the future. But right now, he couldn't ignore a whopping big regret—that he'd never slept with Sarah Richards.

The next day, Sarah folded and refolded a towel in her kitchen while her grandmother sat serenely shaping ground beef into patties to be frozen. Individual patties for lonely meals. Her grandmother and parents invited her to their homes often, or came over to hers like tonight, but nothing could replace the daily companionship of the husband she'd lost.

Tonight, she and Grandma Kat had eaten salads and discussed last-minute details for her grandmother's upcoming sixty-fifth birthday bash this weekend. Yet still Kathleen didn't leave, offering to help with small household chores. Normally, Sarah would have insisted she was fine, but after the day she'd experienced, facing her empty house seemed tougher than normal.

Silently, she worked alongside her grandmother, trying not to think about her lunch shift at the Vista del Mar Beach and Tennis Club. The manager had given her the afternoon off to cool down. She'd been an employee there long enough that she wouldn't get fired—unless Rafe flat-out requested it.

She didn't think he would be that vindictive and he had laughed.

Damn him.

She slammed the towel into the laundry basket, wrecking her stack. "I can't believe he's just going to dismantle the factory, put hundreds of people out of work."

Grandma Kat folded plastic wrap over a perfect circle of hamburger. "I assume you mean Rafe Cameron."

"Who else?" She kicked the wicker hamper to the side. "Even my parents will be out of a job after working at that plant their whole adult lives. Grandma Kat, doesn't this inflame you? Aren't you pissed? You worked for Ronald Worth for forty years. Aren't you hurt to see the place torn apart? Lives destroyed?"

With her parents so close to retirement age, they were too old to start new careers. They'd given up so much for that factory, working long hours and double shifts just to keep a roof over her head. Thank God she'd had Grandma Kat to look after her or she would have been very alone growing up.

"Of course I am upset, dear." She stacked the dozen individually wrapped burgers into a Tupperware container and sealed the lid. "I know the faces and names and histories of all the longtime employees. Thinking of them being out of a job not only makes me mad, it breaks my heart."

Sarah had thought *her* heart couldn't be sliced any deeper than when Rafe moved away after high school graduation, leaving her behind. And then she'd pieced her life together, marrying, creating the home with Quentin that she'd always wanted. Only to have her spirit crushed all over again by multiple miscarriages and then her husband's death.

Truly, she would have thought the calluses on her emotions would leave her immune to pain now. She was wrong.

Tears burned her eyes, blurring her perfect little kitchen. She sagged back against the Formica tabletop she'd loved for its fifties appeal. So much hope had gone into this space. Quentin had repainted the vintage cabinets and wainscoting white while she'd sewn bright chintz curtains and a sink skirt, painting the four chairs bright accent colors.

"I can't believe this is actually happening." Sarah scrubbed her wrist under her eyes, ever aware of her grandmother's perceptive gaze. "I know Rafe blames Worth Industries for his mother's death, but to hang on to that for all these years? That's quite a grudge, especially when there's no proof."

Her grandmother stood up and walked to the ancient refrigerator. She tucked the container full of patties into the freezer. "Heaven knows he was torn up when Hannah died."

When Rafe's dad had decided to remarry near the

end of their senior year, Sarah had been hopeful that he was coming to grips with losing his mother. And recently when she'd heard about the charity he'd created in honor of his mother, she'd thought finally Rafe would find some peace. Hannah's Hope, based in Vista del Mar, was a literacy charity that paired financially disadvantaged individuals with mentors.

Was it really just a promo gig to divert attention from his grudge against Worth Industries or a true testament to making peace with the past? "Do you really think particulates from the factory caused Hannah Cameron's COPD?"

"I honestly don't know who or what to blame for Hannah's tragic death." Kathleen Richards eased back into her chair, slowly, the hint of arthritis the only sign she was slowing down. "Factory safety standards were so different back when she worked there over thirty years ago. And she died nearly sixteen years after she was fired. So it's tough to tell."

"And what about Mom and Dad?" Her parents had worked at the plant for their entire adult lives.

"I do know that Ronald Worth has adhered to safety standards. Were those standards lax? Possibly," she conceded. "Did the man have regrets in his life? Absolutely. But his are more of the personal variety. I would hate to see Rafe suffer that same guilt from letting his private life affect his business decisions."

"You need to tell him that." Sarah reached across the table to clasp her grandmother's hand urgently.

"Do you honestly think Rafe would listen to me?" Kathleen stared back with eyes as green as her own.

"He resented the way I kept tabs on you. If you recall, he and I didn't part on the best of terms."

Sarah snatched her hand away. "And you think he and I did?"

"True enough. The two of you have always evoked strong emotions in each other. Always." Kathleen pinned her with a look stronger than any grip. "I believe you hold sway with him now just as you did then. You are the only person who stands a chance at getting Rafe Cameron to rethink his position on closing the factory."

Her grandmother's words sank in slowly, shockingly. Sarah knew without a doubt Kathleen had come to supper and stayed with a specific agenda. She wanted her granddaughter to use her past connection with Rafe to influence him.

"Grandma, you can't be suggesting I seduce the guy into keeping the factory open?" While her mind, her heart, balked in horror, her body tingled to life at even the suggestion of Rafe's hands on her again. "You vastly oversell my appeal."

"Maybe you undersell yourself. But that's beside the point." Kathleen shook her head, dangling cat earrings swaying. "I would never even suggest anything so crass. I'm simply saying that you and Rafe had a special connection fourteen years ago."

"Whoa, wait." Sarah held up a hand, certain she must have misheard. "You think he and I had a *special* connection? The way I remember it, you were always trying to break the two of us up."

Her grandmother snorted. "I was trying to keep you

from having a baby before you graduated from high school like I did and your parents did."

Sarah stifled the urge to wince over her grandmother's mention of babies, but since her grandmother didn't know about the miscarriages, she couldn't blame her for venturing into painful territory. The first miscarriage had occurred before they'd had a chance to tell anyone, then they'd been wary of sharing news until she made it into her second trimester. That never happened.

There was a time she'd worried her out-of-control passion for Rafe would lead to an accidental pregnancy. Then she'd dreamed of carrying his children. Now she knew she would carry no man's child. "Well, you accomplished your goal, because in spite of all your hints to the contrary, Rafe and I never went far enough to risk that."

In high school, her friends had all assumed she was sleeping with Rafe, but she'd held back, wanting to wait for marriage. Or maybe she'd somehow known from the start they were doomed.

Regardless, how weird was it to be talking to her grandmother about sex?

Kathleen's eyebrows inched toward her hair. "Really? You've surprised even me. The two of you were sneaking around all the time, trying to find time alone."

"That's not fair. We were teenagers dating. Teenagers who also worked long hours after school and had a very, very eagle-eyed grandmother breathing down our necks."

"Hmm, silly me." Kathleen nudged the saltshaker even with the pepper. "I thought dates involved cars and movies, not climbing up a tree to slip into your bedroom."

She gasped, her mind flooding with memories of her and Rafe tangling up in her comforter. "How could you have known that?"

Her grandmother grinned. "I didn't know for sure. Until now."

Sarah sagged back in her seat, weary to her toes from the way Rafe had upset her life all over again. "I can't believe you've reduced me to these word games."

"I just wanted you to be careful then. I could see there was something intense between the two of you, something neither of you were mature enough to deal with yet."

"Well, you were wrong." Her spine steeled with anger even after all these years over how bitterly they'd ended the relationship. "We broke up and moved on. We haven't spoken in fourteen years until today."

"I was there to pick up the pieces when it all fell apart. Everyone in town knows. And if that explosive encounter is anything to judge by, the two of you have some unfinished business of your own."

She pressed her lips tight. What could she say? She agreed. But Rafe hadn't made even a token effort to contact her once he returned. God, she hated how her temper had run away with her today, sucking her into revealing too much of her own unresolved feelings—mostly furious ones—for him. Especially when it was clear he'd moved on.

Kathleen squeezed her hand lightly. "Life is all about timing. You have a chance here to find closure with

Rafe and help the employees at the plant." She clasped her granddaughter's hands. "Talk to him."

As if she had any choice when her grandmother put it like that. And just when she'd thought her heart was numbed from years of scar tissue, she felt a flutter of excitement tickle her ribs at the notion of talking to him again. Without question, one look from Rafe Cameron still sent her body into overdrive. Even if he had turned into the first-class snob he'd sworn he would never become.

With the town's livelihood on the line, she needed to keep her wits about her when dealing with this man, which meant keeping her hormones in check.

Because without question, Rafe had a way of scrambling her thoughts with just one touch.

Sarah stood outside Rafe's office in the Worth Industries building—now Cameron Enterprises—while his secretary checked to make sure he was "available." All high-tech and chrome, the place sure looked up-to-date and safe. It also looked pricey. No refurbished vintage finds around here. This office in Rafe's newly acquired holding was a world away from her tiny house.

When they were teenagers, Rafe had told her more than once that he intended to own this whole town, including a house bigger than Worth's. She'd believed he would become successful, but she'd never envisioned anything like this. She couldn't fathom how he'd made it happen. But then he'd always worked harder and longer hours than anyone she'd known, so much so that finding time for each other had been nearly impossible.

No wonder he'd wanted to leave her behind when he left town. They would have never seen each other. She would have grown frustrated, much as she had when they were dating. A marriage for them would have been destined to fail from the start.

Somehow knowing he'd made the right decision didn't ease the sting of rejection even after all these years.

His office door opened and she jolted. His secretary waved her in without a word, the older woman all crisp efficiency in a wrinkle-free suit. Nerves churning, Sarah refused to feel self-conscious about her simple sundress. Her sandals didn't make a sound as she walked across the plush carpet.

Rafe stood at the window wall with his back to her. The expanse of spot-free glass offered a spectacular view of Vista del Mar, homes and bluffs. Between the tall palms, a distant view of the Pacific Ocean sparkled.

Off to one side in the distance, small stucco houses like hers nestled into a community. On the other, a handful of mansions filled exclusive beach lots.

She'd heard Rafe bought a three-and-a-half-million-dollar condo on the exclusive side of town. How did he feel, finally standing inside Worth Industries and claiming it as his own?

A sentimental corner of her couldn't help cheering for all he'd accomplished. He may have broken her heart, but she'd also loved him. She would let those softer feelings for the boy he'd been help control her temper through this meeting.

She knew he was aware of her entrance even though

he didn't turn, so she waited for his next move. And she had to admit, it was nice to have a second to study him without worrying about him picking up on the attraction she fought so hard to hide. His shoulders filled out the black suit, the fabric so obviously fine she could feel the softness from across the room. Everything from his engraved cuff links to his smooth leather shoes shouted elite, expensive.

And understated.

He might be showing off his wealth for all of Vista del Mar, but he was classy about it.

Finally, he extended an arm and waved her over. Those nerves in her stomach double-timed as she slid into place beside him. Her simple sandals looked so out of place next to imported leather on the Aubusson carpet. There'd been a time when they'd danced barefoot on the beach together.

A million years ago.

She cleared her throat and her mind. "I want to apologize for the way I acted at the Tennis Club. I shouldn't have dumped tea in your lap. I would offer to pay for your dry cleaning, but the Rafe I remember wouldn't let me pay for so much as a soda."

Still, he didn't look at her, just kept staring out over their hometown. "You're apologizing for how you acted but not what you said?"

He wasn't making this easy for her. Once upon a time, she would have just reached for him, threading her fingers through his tawny hair until he shook off his mood and turned toward her.

She tried again. "I'm sorry that I shouted at you in front of a roomful of people."

"Interesting to note that you *still* haven't taken back what you said, only the way and place you said it."

Okay, so much for the dignified approach. Less than a minute together and he was already making her angry. "Why have you ignored me since you returned to town?"

"I didn't think you would want to speak to me," he said simply. "Isn't that what you said the last time we spoke? Something like, 'I'm going to get out of the car now and I do not want you to follow me. I'm going to call my grandmother for a ride. And I mean it. I don't want to see you again.'"

That was exactly what she'd said. Verbatim. That he remembered after all this time, that she remembered, rocked her. Too much.

"I was an eighteen-year-old girl in the middle of a drama queen meltdown." She'd issued ridiculous ultimatums out of fear, and also out of a certainty that he would follow her. She'd been wrong. "We're both adults now."

"You're right." Turning, he faced her. His features might look familiar but the calculating gleam in his blue eyes was new and unsettling. "You came here for a reason, now let's get to it."

She tipped her chin and refused to let him intimidate her. "I want to make it up to you for how I behaved. How about a home-cooked meal?"

His blue eyes narrowed suspiciously. "You are asking me to dinner?"

"For old time's sake." Because she needed to help her family. And because she couldn't deny she needed some of that peace for herself when it came to how they'd left things between them after graduation. "An olive branch in the interest of declaring a truce."

"At your place?"

"Seven o'clock at my house, yes." Where she'd lived with Quentin Dobbs. No man other than relatives had set foot in her home since he died. She swallowed down a swell of emotion. "I'm not a five-star chef by any means, but I grill a great steak and my backyard atmosphere can't be beat. For old time's sake," she repeated.

Impulsively, she thrust out her hand and then felt silly standing there while she waited for him to take it.

Or worse yet, waiting for him to reject it, reject her.

His hands slid from behind his back and enfolded hers in his. His fingers closed over where she wore her wedding band on her right hand these days, since she'd lost Quentin. Was it her imagination or did Rafe's thumb press harder against the silver band?

She'd loved Quentin, deeply. Yes, that love had been different from what she and Rafe shared, different but still special. She missed Quentin and the simple life they'd built every single day.

So why did she ache to squeeze Rafe's hand and tug him closer? Something flashed in his eyes, but skittered through so fast she didn't have time to analyze it before it was gone.

The heat of his skin warmed her for an instant before he let go.

"I'll see you at seven o'clock then."

"Great." She backed away, reaching behind her for the door. "We'll finally have a chance to talk and catch up on everything."

Her grip closed around the doorknob and she exhaled

hard with relief. She'd made it through this encounter easier than she'd expected. Maybe talking to Rafe tonight wouldn't be so difficult after all.

"Sarah?"

His voice stopped her dead and made her skin tingle with nerves. She glanced back over her shoulder. "Yes?"

"Skip the steak. I'd rather have a cheeseburger."

His arrogant grin told her he knew full well the reference would bring reminders of that first night he'd climbed through her bedroom window, and other stolen moments of picnic meals and frantic make-out sessions. Rafe may not have spoken to her since he returned to Vista del Mar, but it was clear he hadn't forgotten the past any more than she had. Fourteen years ago she'd trusted Rafe not to hurt her and he'd trampled all over her feelings and dreams.

This time, she wouldn't be so naive.

She recognized the light in his eyes too well. The same blue-hot flame had blazed over her whenever he'd vowed he wanted nothing more than to bury himself heart-deep inside her. And though she felt the same passion coursing through her veins, she'd held back then, even when she'd loved him.

She would sure as hell hold back tonight.

Three

Rafe leaned against his desk as Sarah made tracks out of his office. She may have invited him to her place for supper, but he suffered no delusions that she wished to rekindle their old flame.

Business instincts blared that she wanted to convince him to leave what remained of Worth Industries intact. And she would fail. She couldn't succeed in diverting him from revenge now any more than she had in the past. But he was still curious just how far she would go to persuade him.

Sundress swishing around her slim legs, she angled sideways out the door being held open by Chase on his way in. His stepbrother nodded politely, then turned his attention toward Rafe. Chase didn't even bother hiding his curiosity as an eyebrow shot up.

At least he waited until Sarah stepped into the elevator before speaking.

Turning back, Chase asked, "What's she doing here? Sounded to me like she said her piece back at the restaurant yesterday."

Rafe closed the office door again, the floral scent of Sarah lingering in his space. "Apparently not."

"At least you managed to stay dry this time." Chase dropped into a black leather chair by the sofa, sliding a portfolio onto the coffee table. "Does this mean the two of you are rekindling the old flame?"

Rafe forced himself to sit in the seat across from Chase rather than pacing around, broadcasting how restless one visit from Sarah left him. "Just because you're wallowing in marital bliss with Emma doesn't mean you have to haul the rest of us down with you."

While they shared the same business drive, they differed in their personal lives. Rafe kept dating low-key, fostering easy relationships with corporate women who had as little free time as he did. Chase had been more of a player until settling down with Emma Worth. The former playboy was now a proud papa-to-be.

Chase thumbed his own wedding band absently. "I know how far gone you were on Sarah Richards back in the day. I could see it whenever I came out to visit Mom, and I barely even knew you."

"Back in the day, sure." He'd loved her then, or thought he had. He couldn't deny he was still attracted to her. But that's all it was. "Not now."

"That's not how it seemed at lunch. Sparks were flying."

"That was me flying out of my chair when she soaked my lap."

Chase chuckled. "Priceless moment."

"Glad you're amused." He tapped the monogrammed portfolio in front of him. "Do you think we could stop gossiping about my love life and focus on business?"

"She's single. You're single," Chase said without so much as reaching for the graphs Rafe spread out on the coffee table. "What's to stop you from following those sparks?"

"Did you not hear me, my brother? We're here to work."

"No need to start without Preston and Tanner." Both men were top-level executives, part of the very small inner circle of the trusted few in his own personal Dream Team.

Rafe looked sideways at his stepbrother. "You're a real pain in the ass today."

"You're extraordinarily crabby yourself, and I think we both know the root of your bad mood." Chase leaned forward, elbows on his knees. "She could only bother you this much if she still means something to you."

A damned good point and Chase was the only one who could say it. Rafe would have flat-out denied the claim from anyone else. "I'm seeing her tonight for supper. Now can we get to work?"

"Dinner date? Where are you taking her? I hear Jacques' keeps a table reserved for you all the time now."

Just the mention of the exclusive French restaurant stoked his bad mood even more. Back when they'd been teenagers, he'd planned to take her there for Valentine's

Day. Then the electric company had been ready to shut off their power. His dad had been flat broke from paying off medical bills even three years after Hannah's death. Rafe hadn't hesitated to pay the bill, which meant no special Valentine's date.

He'd settled for taking her to the beach with a picnic meal his dad's fiancée had cooked. Fourteen years later, his pride still stung over how little he'd been able to give Sarah then. "I thought you were my business manager, not my social secretary."

"I'm your brother and your friend." Chase pinned him with an intuitive look as effective as any wrestling neck lock they may have resorted to as teens. "I know you better than anyone. Even your old man doesn't know half the things about you that I do. There's an edge to you lately and it's not good. Is it so wrong that I want to see you happy?"

"Once the changeover is complete, I'll be very happy."

Chase opened his mouth to respond only to be cut short by a knock.

"Come in," Rafe called, so ready to end this conversation he didn't much care who walked through the door.

Luckily for him, the rest of the Dream Team had arrived—Preston and Tanner. Max Preston, his public relations guru, came from old California money. However, despite his privileged upbringing and inheritance, he never depended on it. Max was a real go-getter who'd never met an image crisis he couldn't solve. Max would be moving on soon to devote his time fully to charity foundation work, but for now, Rafe intended to make the most of his input here.

Next through the door was William Tanner, CFO of Cameron Enterprises. The New Zealander was unflinchingly ruthless in the business world, the only individual Rafe had ever met who was equally as hardnosed—all the more reason to make sure Tanner worked on the Cameron team.

Rafe shifted into business mode, on the outside at least, going through the motions of starting the PowerPoint slides on breaking down the redistribution of Worth Industry assets. But he knew his mind was only half in the game today.

Already Sarah proved a distraction in the workplace. Because in spite of the high-profile presentation flashing on the screen in front of him, Rafe could only think of the upcoming dinner at her place. Even the thought of seeing her ramped anticipation inside him. Ignoring her hadn't worked for the past five months, much less for the past fourteen years.

The time had come to take a more proactive approach to working Sarah Richards out of his system, once and for all.

Doorbell echoing through her two-bedroom stucco home, Sarah wiped her hands on a dish towel, checked the throw pillows on her rattan sofa, straightened a rag scatter rug with her toe even though she knew everything was perfectly in place. Her house might not be on as grand a scale as Rafe's these days, but she took pride in every perfectly maintained square foot.

The bell rang again and she drop-kicked the hand

towel out of sight under the sofa before opening the door. Rafe stood on the tiny porch beside a potted cactus. He wore jeans and a black polo shirt that likely cost more than her couch, but the less formal clothes made him seem more approachable, more like the boy she'd known all those years ago.

Although the five-o'clock shadow and perfect blue-jeans butt were far more manly than boyish. What did he think of her denim shorts and layered tank tops? She hadn't wanted to dress up and seem like she was trying to impress. But of course her pride cared that he would eat his heart out over dumping her.

"Come in." Her voice came out raspy and she swallowed fast before trying again. "Supper's ready to go on the grill."

Stepping aside for him to come inside, she noticed the bouquet in his hand. Oh God. Her stomach flipped faster than any burger on a grill as she remembered all the blooms he'd given her while they dated. He'd been short of cash in those days, yet somehow he'd always managed to bring her flowers.

Tonight, he'd chosen orchids, a mix of pinks and purples so gorgeous her fingers itched to gather them up to her nose.

"Thank you," she said simply, suddenly nervous about being alone with him and all these memories. How had she let her grandmother talk her into this?

Expensive flowers clutched to her chest, she couldn't help but see her home through his eyes. No doubt her little house could fit into his whole master bedroom.... And wait, how had her thoughts gone to his bedroom?

Quietly, Rafe followed her into the kitchen. They'd

never lacked for things to talk about, had only needed more free time to say it all. Now, her mouth dried right up as she filled a glass pitcher for the flowers. She didn't have a vase. She and Quentin had poured every extra penny into fixing up their home. And he hadn't been the sort to bring flowers and chocolates anyway. He'd bought her new windows and light fixtures….

She and Quentin had purchased the house with the intent of starting a family. They'd repainted and decorated every room together, except the spare bedroom. She'd delayed any work on that space, planning to make it a nursery. Why paint it one color only to have to change it once the baby arrived?

Except there wasn't a baby. Even after nine years of marriage and trips to a fertility specialist that had stripped every penny of their savings, there never was a baby. Three miscarriages in her first trimester. The last one occurred after the car wreck that took Quentin's life.

Water overflowed from the pitcher. Gasping, she turned off the brushed-nickel faucet—an anniversary gift from Quentin—and carefully placed the flowers inside. Too bad the emotions swelled inside her until she felt like that glass container, unable to contain it all.

Putting on her best game face, she turned back to Rafe. "Let's go to the backyard. There's a nice breeze tonight."

"Lead the way." His footsteps echoed behind her on the freshly scrubbed linoleum, then on the stone walkway outside.

Her garden haven spread in front of her, enclosed with a wooden plank fence.

After Quentin and her third unborn baby died, she'd devoted herself to cultivating the outdoor space. While Quentin had been gifted with a hammer, he'd never had a green thumb. She couldn't bring herself to sell the house, but she found herself hiding out here more and more. She'd been driven to create something, anything alive and bright in a world so horribly full of death. She'd chosen sturdy plants at first, cacti putting down roots around a fountain. Finding her confidence and her footing, she'd added lemon and orange trees for shade.

She set the pitcher of orchids in the middle of the wrought iron table set for two.

Rafe walked to the center of the yard, turning slowly. He whistled low. "The landscaping is fantastic."

"Quentin was good with that." The lie rolled off her lips, so much easier than the truth that she'd hidden from her house. And yes, maybe she wanted to see how Rafe would react to a mention of her husband. "He drew up the blueprint right before he died."

He stopped stone-still, his eyes sliding from the fountain—a terra-cotta pot pouring water over piles of polished stones—back up to her. "I'm sorry for your loss."

Dozens of people had said those same words, that same pat line, and yet for some reason it grated on her already raw nerves coming from Rafe. "You're a bit late with the condolences."

"Did you expect to hear from me three years ago?"

She'd expected to hear from him fourteen years ago after he'd left town. Never had she dreamed one fight could erase all they'd shared. She'd hoped for some word, a letter, a call for an entire year before she'd given up and moved on with her life.

But she wouldn't let herself be that vulnerable around this man. "After Quentin died, I heard from your father and Penny, and they came to the funeral."

His blue eyes held her, stroked her, tangibly touched her without him moving so much as a step closer. "You're too damn young to be a widow."

She wrapped her arms around herself defensively. "There's never a good time to lose someone you love."

"You loved him then," he said, his voice emotionless, his face inscrutable.

"I married him." She pivoted away from those probing eyes and turned on the electric grill. "I wouldn't have married him unless I loved him."

"Teenagers change their minds a lot that way."

She glanced over her shoulder. "I don't care for veiled references. If you have something to say, just say it. I know you can't be jealous. So what is all of this about?"

He stalked closer, stopping just shy of the grill and picking up the container from the open ice chest. "You're the one who invited me over," he said, passing her the raw patties, "for cheeseburgers."

She snatched the plastic dish from him, her temper already frothing to life in spite of her best intentions.

Rafe stared back at her silently as if they were just old friends catching up. Well, that would have worked if he'd contacted her once he returned to town. She could have pretended she was okay with everything, that it was all water under the bridge. But the way he'd ignored her for the past five months poured salt on some very old wounds.

Still, he said nothing, damn him.

"Yes, I loved him. And yes, I loved you before that. So what? You chose to leave town and you chose to let one argument wipe out everything else. What was I supposed to do? Mope around all infatuated with you for the rest of my life? I may not have left Vista del Mar, but I moved on when it came to living my life."

He nodded once, a smile tucking into his face if not up to his eyes. "You always did have a way of putting me in my place."

"Somebody needs to," she said under her breath, peeling a ground-beef patty up and onto the grill, the meat sizzling. She dropped two more beside it.

"Is that why you invited me over, to put me in my place?" He sat at the table, extending his legs in front of him.

Long, lean legs that made her mouth water.

God, how had she lost sight of her real reason for asking him over? Lowering the flame, she closed the grill and sat across from him carefully. She needed to change the tone of the conversation fast, because they very obviously hadn't reached a point where they could talk about personal stuff.

"Actually, I wanted to talk about Worth Industries."

"It's not Worth Industries anymore."

"Right, of course. And that's just my point, the take-over. Rafe, I know you've always been ambitious, but the person I knew all those years ago wouldn't be so heartless. It's not too late for you or for the factory. Production has slowed but the place isn't completely shut down. You can still change your mind." She reached across the table, reached out to him. "The man who started Hannah's Hope couldn't do something like this. What's really going on?"

"The factory is outdated." His hand moved closer to hers, so near she thought he would clasp hers. Then he skimmed past and pulled an orchid from the pitcher. "If I keep it open, I'm only delaying the inevitable. Better to rip the bandage off fast."

"That's not going to be much consolation to my parents as they lose their jobs." Her hands fisted on the cool iron, the scent of other barbecues on the breeze as she forced herself to breathe deeply, control her temper.

"My legal staff and I worked out retirement packages for long-term employee of Worth Industries."

"For half of what they'd been expecting before." Mist from the neighbor's sprinkler carried over the fence but did little to cool her mood.

"They may have been promised more but it wasn't feasible." He skimmed the fragile bloom over her tight fist until her fingers unfurled. "The funds would have dried up within five years of retirement."

"Says you." She snatched her flower from him and sagged back in her chair.

"It doesn't really matter whether you believe me or not," he said arrogantly. "I'm giving you a courtesy explanation. I did not ask for your input."

"You never did want my opinion, not when it mattered most." The words fell out of her mouth before she could stop them, but damn it, he'd lied to her.

They'd made a plan for the future. She'd been willing to leave Vista del Mar for him if they could get married.

Only he'd wanted to go to Los Angeles, a huge city and the last sort of place where she could be happy. And she'd realized he didn't really want to marry her, but had just felt pressured. Even thinking about that time made her feel edgy and raw. Too often she used her temper to hide hurt

She hadn't meant to say something so vulnerable to him tonight, but then her temper always had made her mouth run away.

Well, her temper or tequila. Since she wasn't drinking tonight, it had to be her temper. The burgers sizzled behind her.

"Sounds to me like you're holding a hefty grudge for someone who's moved on with her life." He nudged aside the pitcher of flowers and leaned onto the small table, closer to her. "Maybe you still have feelings for me after all."

Feelings? Of course she did and that made her mad as hell. She hated this out-of-control feeling inside her. She was every bit as hormonal around him now as she had been when they were teens. "If you count anger and frustration as 'feelings' then yes."

"We were very good at the frustration part back in the day." He shifted from his seat to stand beside her, leaning against the table, close, too close. "And I'm willing to admit that when I'm next to you—" his hand closed around hers holding the orchid "—seeing you, breathing in the scent of you, I'm frustrated all over again."

His admission sent a fresh wash of arousal gushing through her veins.

"Sucks to be you." Too bad her bravado was betrayed by her trembling hand.

"You're irritable." His voice rumbled over her, silky-smooth as the hint of his aftershave. "Abstinence always did make you cranky."

"I'm not cranky and I'm not abstinent," she lied. Her breasts pebbled with awareness, an aching need gathering between her legs. She snatched her hand away.

His calf brushed against her knee. He pulled the orchid from her fingers and tucked the bloom behind her ear. "And here I thought I was turning you on."

"Not in the least." *Liar.*

Three years of abstinence ate her all the more fiercely now with temptation a hand's stretch away.

His smile spread again, full out this time, all the way to his sexy blue eyes. "Care to test that out, Kitten?"

Four

Rafe couldn't tamp down the need to kiss Sarah.

Here. Now. On her garden patio. In a place where she'd lived for years with her husband. Quentin Dobbs might be dead, but he'd also stepped in the minute Rafe left town. Sarah had chosen Dobbs, been with Dobbs. Even the thought of that twisted his gut more than it should.

No doubt, the driving need hammering through him came from some lingering territorial urge to claim her as his. They had unfinished business, he and Sarah, and he wasn't going to throw away this chance to settle things between them.

His mouth covered hers, firmly, surely.

For the first time since they'd been teens, he kissed her. Not as hard or deep as he burned to do, but he couldn't mess this up by going Cro-Magnon right out of the gate. He'd learned in business a long time ago that success was often determined in the first moments of any transaction.

And he definitely wanted this transaction to succeed.

She went stock-still against him in surprise, so quiet he could vow he heard her heart racing even more loudly than the *click, click, click* of the neighbor's sprinkler. Then a sigh slipped between her lips, all the encouragement he needed. Thoughts of business transactions scattered.

Need, pure and undiluted, seared him, drove him. He plunged his fingers into her loose hair, the orchid tumbled away, releasing a burst of perfume and a surge of desire. The fragrances from her garden laced the air with more memories of their teenage years, blooms crushed between them in a frantic clutch.

Hands trailing down her back, he pressed her more closely to him. Each curve against him made his fingers burn to peel away her clothes and rediscover her more mature—somehow unbelievably more sexy shape.

He. Wanted. Her.

The minute he'd stepped out here and she'd said her dead husband planned this place, Rafe had almost lost it thinking about some other guy giving her all these flowers. Flowers had been their gig back when they'd dated, the only nice thing he'd been able to give her.

And he'd only been able to manage that by swallowing his pride and working at the Worth greenhouse before school. Actually, he'd been hired by the gardener, Juan Rodriguez, but all the same he'd shoveled manure in the early morning haze for Sarah. He'd stumbled onto the job in an attempt to get her a bouquet for Valentine's Day. Then once he'd seen how nuts she went over a few blossoms he couldn't even name, he'd kept on shoveling.

In those days, he would have done just about anything to see Sarah smile. Anything except stay in this lame-ass little town.

The past clawing at his brain, he searched her mouth more fully. His hands roved down, down farther still over her hips. His fingertips grazed the hem of her shorts, the start of the creamy bare flesh of her legs. Her moan ricocheted through him, pulling a groan from deep in his gut.

Her nails dug into his back with the same kittenish sharp claws of want he remembered well during the darkest part of the night when he allowed himself to think about Sarah. To want Sarah. To plot how someday he would buy the whole town and her along with it.

Except when he'd come back, he'd seen she hadn't changed one bit. Sarah's small-town heart and hometown values still weren't for sale.

The taste of her flooded his senses until he went rock-hard, aching to be inside her. Just her. Hell, he hadn't even been able to kiss another woman for eighteen months after he'd left this place, and he'd only done it then because he'd heard about Sarah's engagement to Quentin Dobbs. A guy they'd known all through school. A genuinely nice fella who'd never made a secret of the fact that he wanted Sarah too.

Now, Rafe stood in Dobbs's garden, with Dobbs's wife, and the guy was dead, which made it even tougher.

Because he couldn't face him, man to man, and win her away from him.

His hands on the silky skin of her thighs, her hands in his hair, his body throbbed to claim her, to finally understand what it was about this woman that made her so damn unforgettable. Fingers grazing upward, he tugged at the hem of her layered tank tops, exploring the soft expanse of her back—

Sarah pulled away abruptly, gasping, her lips full and moist illuminated by the backyard floodlight. "No..." She held up a trembling hand. "No..."

And he wasn't surprised by her pulling away. Sarah had been sending out mixed signals from the day they'd started dating.

She'd vowed then that she loved him, had said she would leave Vista del Mar with him. But once he got down to specifics for relocating, she'd freaked out. She would point to every tiny town on the map and sing its praises until he realized even if she left, she would only be happy in a Vista del Mar clone.

He'd even offered to marry her, though the prospect had scared the crap out of him. Then, she'd bailed on him at the last second. He'd lasted two years before he'd crumbled like a damn fool and come back for her. Except she'd gotten over him mighty damn fast. A year after he'd left, she started dating Quentin, then married him a year after that.

Rafe jammed his fists into his pockets.

Kneeling quickly, she picked the flower off the ground and set it carefully on the table. "This isn't why I invited you over tonight."

"Are you so sure of that?"

"Of course I am." She grabbed the back of the patio chair for balance as she swayed. "I was recruited to talk to you about the plant."

"Recruited?" Damn. Her words splashed proverbial cold water all over his libido as effectively as if that neighboring sprinkler hit him dead on. "Of course you were."

He'd already figured out she wanted to change his mind. But he'd never thought others would try to use her to influence him. Somehow the people around him had perceived her as a weakness in his armor and that couldn't be tolerated.

Stepping closer, he studied her mussed hair and defensive eyes reflecting the starlight. "You can save your breath, Sarah." He hated Ronald Worth for what the man had done to his family. "No one will ever convince me that my mother didn't develop COPD from conditions at that plant. Even if Worth didn't known the problem existed, he still fired my mother and father once she got pregnant."

Citing B.S. fraternization rules. Hannah and Bob had been out of their jobs, no insurance, with a baby on the way. They'd never recovered from that financial setback. Later, his mother had known she was sick long before she'd gone to a doctor, putting off visits to save money.

And then it had been too late.

A car rumbled into the neighbor's driveway as Rafe held back angry words. His jaw clenched as he wrestled with his fury—at Ronald Worth and with whoever had set Sarah up tonight.

"Sarah, no matter how much I want you, I'm not going to lose sight of my goal here."

She gasped. "Are you accusing me of seducing you on purpose?"

The thought hadn't crossed his mind, until now. Her obvious anger knocked that notion clear out of the running. "No, I'm accusing other people of bargaining on my obvious attraction to you."

She chewed her kissed-plump bottom lip, then drew in a shaky breath. "I would have spoken to you about this anyway. The way you're acting, the things you're doing don't make sense. You're confusing me. You seem so familiar and so very different all at once."

"I'm the same man I've always been."

"I can almost believe that sometimes." She turned away quickly, opening the grill and releasing the smoky scent. Exasperation radiated off her as tangible as the heat waves rolling from the flames.

"Then trust your instincts." Especially if they would lead her—finally—into his bed.

She flipped the burgers, pulled out thick slices of cheddar cheese and placed them on top, keeping her back to him, her hands busy with nervous activity. "You seem genuine in your dedication to Hannah's Hope. In the short time the charity has been in Vista del Mar, it's improved morale, and improved so many lives—everywhere I look, people are signing up for additional schooling, volunteering and really raising the overall quality of life in our community."

"And that's a problem why?"

Sighing, she closed the grill heavily. "How can I—how can you—reconcile the man who does so much good with the one who is singlehandedly destroying the livelihoods of hundreds of people?"

Her hands dropped to her sides, nothing left to do in tending the meal. Her head fell forward, and she eyed him sideways, strangely uncertain for outspoken Sarah. "Is the boy I remember, the one I fell in love with, the one who had big dreams of making a difference with his millions, still there? Does any part of him still exist?"

Was that hope or condemnation in her voice?

Regardless, he wasn't going to argue with her about his business practices or provide some kind of spreadsheet of jobs created, charitable contributions made. He hadn't cracked the Forbes 400 by the time he was thirty to now start justifying his way of doing business. He was here for something different tonight. "There's one way to find out what you want to know about me."

She faced him fully, slowly, warily. "If you think we're going to kiss again—or more—you can forget it."

Damn, but he liked seeing her spunk return. "Spend time with me."

"Excuse me?" Her eyes went wide.

"Go out on dates with me." He clasped her shoulders. "Give me the chance to follow through on all the places I vowed I would take you."

"Whoa, hold on." She started to place her hands on his chest then stopped an inch shy, which said a helluva lot more than if she'd hadn't thought twice about the contact. She backed up a step. "You're suggesting we just pick up where we left off? That's impossible."

He stalked closer. "I'm stating, that if you want to change my mind about Worth Industries, then here's your chance. Complete and unfettered access to my undivided attention."

She hesitated, but didn't say no. "For how long?"

"If you convince me tomorrow, then so be it." But he knew she wouldn't.

She snorted on a laugh and reached for the spatula. "Somehow I don't think that's going to happen."

"Okay, how about this?" He settled on a quick compromise, one that gave him the window of time he needed to seal the deal, to finally get Sarah Richards into his bed. "Everybody's been buzzing about your grandmother's birthday bash coming up at the end of the week. We both have this week to present our case as to why or why not the plant should remain open. We can start with dinner tomorrow night."

Eyeing him suspiciously, she toyed with the spatula for a second before returning to the grill, pulling off the burgers and placing them on an Aztec pottery plate. "I'm busy tomorrow."

She was a rotten liar. Always had been.

But he could let it slide since he would win in the end. "Dinner the next evening then, at Jacques', and we will spend time together every day after that."

Keeping the plate firmly between them, she chewed her bottom lip. "We go on a few dates and that's all? We just spend time together? We're going to talk about keeping Worth Industries open?"

He took the plate from her hands and set it on the table. Clasping her shoulders, he stared straight into her beautiful, confused green eyes.

"You aren't listening to me, Kitten. I said we'll each present our case. *You* can talk about the plant." His thumb stroked the quickening pulse in her neck. "*I,* on the other hand, am going convince you to have the night of uninhibited sex we denied ourselves fourteen years ago."

Driving toward the Worth mansion to pick up her grandmother from a meeting, Sarah didn't know what she was going to tell Grandma Kat about her discussion with Rafe. And no doubt, tenacious Kathleen Richards would push for answers about how the previous evening had gone.

After his outrageous proposal about working his way into her bed, he'd backed off and eaten his burger. But his eyes had devoured her even more effectively than he'd downed his supper. Then he'd said a polite good-night, without so much as touching or kissing her again.

She tossed and turned all night long, aching from that single moment, remembering all too clearly the first time he'd ever kissed her. He'd surprised her by picking her up after work so she wouldn't have to take the bus so late at night. They'd driven around, ended up at the local make-out spot, Busted Bluff.

They'd both grown up in Vista del Mar. However, their contact had been limited up until then. Rafe had always been aloof, even as a second-grader on the playground, even more so as a brooding teen who'd lost his mother.

But that night in January of their senior year, the first night they'd gone out together, everything had changed....

* * *

Reclining in the back of Rafe's El Camino, she soaked up the moonlight, the stars and the chance to finally be alone with a guy she'd fantasized about for years.

He pressed his lips against the racing pulse in her wrist, right over where she'd broken it in the second grade. "I'm sorry I wasn't nicer to you that day on the playground."

Her hand shook. God, all of her insides quivered from the feel of his mouth on her. "You're forgiven."

"Thanks, Sarah...." His smile caressed the sensitive inside of her wrist.

Then his hands stroked higher, up her arms until he cupped the back of her neck. Finally, thank goodness, finally, his head dipped toward her, blocking out the moon and all of Vista del Mar until it was just her and him in their own little world.

He slanted his mouth against hers, more gently than she would have expected. He was such a guy of tough angles, attitude and even bitterness. But right now, she felt all the good in him she'd hoped—known—was there.

The stroke of his tongue along the seam of her lips was the only encouragement she needed. She locked her arms around his neck and committed her all to the kiss. She tested the glide of his hair through her fingers, mussing it the way she'd imagined doing so many times. This was the Rafe in her dreams, the man in her diary fantasies.

She'd told herself it was just a high school crush. A really-long-held high school crush that only her grandmother had guessed. He wasn't her type. He wasn't even attainable, this brooding guy who only went out with girls who dressed all in black.

But she didn't want to think about the other people he'd dated. She didn't want to think about her grandmother's warnings to set her sights on another boy.

Tonight, Rafe was here with her. Kissing her. Stroking up and down her back in a way that sent goose bumps prickling along her skin. Making her ache to press closer and demand more from the kiss, from the moment, from him.

The buttons of his jean jacket pressed into her flesh as she burrowed closer. Her hands parted his coat and twisted in his T-shirt.

And then suddenly cool air was rushing between them. Rafe had pulled away. His chest pumped fast, his hand heavy on her shoulder. It was as if he was keeping distance between them, but couldn't totally let her go.

She struggled to get her bearings, but the lights of Vista del Mar swirled on the horizon. She loosened her hold on his T-shirt and smoothed the wrinkles she put in the body-warmed cotton.

Oh my. Muscles.

His low growl of pleasure rumbled under her fingertips. Her nails dug in lightly.

"Ah, Kitten, this isn't smart," *he said softly, hauling her against his chest anyway.*

He was breathing every bit as fast as she was. His heart hammered under her ear. She swallowed hard against the kick of relief. The crazy way she felt wasn't one-sided. He wanted her too.

She might be reckless for coming here with him. Her

grandmother would chew her out, ground her, lecture her into infinity if she found out.

But she couldn't ignore the hopeful voice whispering in her head that maybe all her late-night fantasies about Rafe, about them together could come true....

Sarah startled back to the present as she reached the front entrance of the Worth mansion and stopped her little Kia Rio. Her fantasies about Rafe hadn't come true then and they sure as hell hadn't played out last night.

He'd left her standing extremely confused and supremely sexually frustrated on her front doorstep. Her very small doorstep, especially in comparison to the Spanish-style mansion looming in front of her.

Turning off her econo car, she eyed all the arches and windows that offered a kabillion-dollar view of the Pacific. Decked out with a pool and tennis courts, the place sported all the luxury Rafe used to talk about "giving" her one day.

But it was the magnificent gardens that drew her eye most.

She switched off the engine and tossed her keys onto the seat. Stepping from the car, she scanned the grotto area of the garden. Palm trees rustled overhead. She was supposed to meet her grandmother here. Kathleen should have finished her meeting with the Worths' family chef about last-minute details for catering her big birthday party—Ronald Worth's gift to Kathleen as his longtime assistant.

"May I help you, Mrs. Dobbs?"

She spun around quickly and followed the heavily accented voice to...Juan Rodriguez. Tucked just behind a horse fountain, he pruned a vine climbing artfully along a patio wall.

Sarah had visited the estate often over the years, and she'd learned a lot from Mr. Worth's head gardener, Juan Rodriguez. Mr. Rodriguez had retired years ago, but he still puttered around his old workspace, checking over the newer help's job tending the space he'd nurtured to such manicured magnificence.

Mrs. Dobbs, he'd called her. He always spoke so formally, and he'd never quite grasped her return to her maiden name a year after Quentin died.

"I'm just Sarah, Mr. Rodriguez." She stepped deeper into the grotto area, the scent of tropical blooms and salt water seeping through her and almost smoothing her knotted nerves.

"Of course," he said, studying her with his wise way that always seemed to see deeper than the surface. "And are you lost?"

"I was supposed to pick up my grandmother and she told me she would be waiting in the garden after she spoke with the chef, but I don't see her."

"I believe she's still inside, speaking with Mr. Worth. They should be finished soon."

"Thank you." She gestured to the sculpted land-scaping around her, a bed of succulents profuse and self-reliant on the bank near her feet. "Your garden is stunning."

"It is not mine anymore, but the staff here lets me pretend I am still in charge on occasion." He looked down at his overalls with a chagrined smile. "I hear from my Ana that yours is quite a showpiece as well."

His daughter Ana headed Hannah's Hope. The old

guy made no secret of his pride in his only child. When Ana was hired for the position, Sarah had wondered if maybe Rafe was interested in her. But Ana was now engaged to musical superstar Ward Miller.

Engagements and weddings and pregnancies were cropping up faster than anything she planted in her barren love life. Except she had that impending date with Rafe tomorrow night....

She shifted her focus back to Mr. Rodriguez. "My garden is nothing like what you've created here."

"Ana tells me differently from when she attended the engagement shower you hosted for Margaret Tanner. She told me that your backyard is magnificent."

Having a party for friends who were married to millionaires had felt...strange, given she had to clip coupons to make ends meet. But damn it all, she was proud of her home, and once everyone arrived, she realized her friends hadn't become different people just because their bank balances increased. She'd tossed some tiny white lights in the trees and stuck to a simple cake, fruit and punch menu. The garden party and bridal shower had been a wonderful surprise hit. Wealth didn't have to change everybody.

Could Rafe learn that lesson as well?

"Mr. Rodriguez, do you have any suggestions for growing bougainvillea?" The shrub should grow in paper-thin, jewel-tone bracts around petite white flowers. Hers just kept drying up and dying.

"Timing, it is all about timing, patience and determination." He dusted his hands off on his overalls. "You do not want to miss the prime window for planting and nurturing. I would be happy to come by sometime and offer suggestions if you would like."

"Thank you. I would appreciate that very much." She backed away. "I'll go find my grandmother now. Have a nice day."

She turned toward the stone path leading to the gargantuan front door.

"Mrs. Dobbs?" Mr. Rodriguez called out.

Pivoting, she found the older gardener had his Zen look turned up to full wattage. "Yes, sir?"

"Here." He extended his hand, holding a hibiscus, and not just any hibiscus, but an exotic orange sherbet-colored one.

"Gracias," she said, taking the flower, the lush fragrance reminding her of supper with Rafe in her backyard.

Reminding her of kissing Rafe.

Climbing the steps to the huge front doors, she roped in her wayward thoughts and focused on retrieving her grandmother. Grandma Kat had finely tuned radar and if Sarah so much as thought of how Rafe had turned her inside out, she would be facing a serious question-and-answer drill session.

She smiled at the butler as he waved her inside toward the library before disappearing into the dining room. The place was impressive, no doubt, but a little cold and too "perfect" for her.

Her red flip-flops slapped imported Italian marble floors. The walls were crammed with original artwork that Mr. Worth was rumored to have traveled the world to acquire. Voices drifted out into the hall from the library. The door was only cracked a bit, but enough, especially with the foyer's high ceiling bouncing around words like racquet balls.

"Ronald," Kathleen Richards said, her voice unmistakable, "you need to speak with Rafe, to tell him the truth and clear the air before it's too late."

Sarah stopped short. She hated to eavesdrop, but once Rafe's name entered the mix, she couldn't make herself back away or push the door open to stop the conversation. Tell Rafe what, exactly?

"I know you're right, Kathleen," Ronald Worth said heavily, wearily, "but I haven't worked up the courage yet."

Sarah pressed her back to the stairway, frozen by a priceless urn on a stand.

"Well," her grandmother continued from the other room, "it's been five months since he returned to town, my friend. I think it's about time to quit waiting for the courage or the perfect moment and just talk."

"He's not the only one who would be affected by learning the truth. I have to take into account how to tell the others."

"They have a right to know as well."

The sound of footsteps above, moving toward the top of the stairs startled her. She glanced up quickly and found a maid descending, dusting the tops of framed art.

Sarah stepped away from the urn toward the library and knocked. Her light tap jarred the door open. Her grandmother and Ronald Worth stood close to each other by rows of books. He was pinching the bridge of his nose.

Clearing her throat, Sarah stepped into the open doorway. "Hello?"

They jolted apart. Grandma Kat clutched her purse to her chest and Ronald Worth's hand fell away from his face, though worry lines furrowed his distinguished brow.

"Grandma?" She stepped into the room tentatively. "Are you ready to go? We have that appointment over at the Tennis Club about where you want the tables and the cabana set up."

"Of course, dear." She hurried to her granddaughter's side, low heels clicking on the floor.

"Mr. Worth," Sarah said, nodding tightly, not one hundred percent comfortable around this guy. Maybe it had something to do with how Rafe felt about him. But she also couldn't deny the twinge of sympathy over all the man had lost—his wife, his company. "I hope you're having a nice day."

"Forced into retirement?" He snorted. "There's nothing but lounging around now."

Her grandmother shook her head. "You should stop being a workaholic and spend time with your children." Grandma Kat took Sarah's arm and started toward the door. "Family should be cherished and nurtured."

Sarah winced in pain, thinking about all the great-grandchildren she'd hoped to give Grandma Kat. She'd clawed her way through the grief these past three years. But moments like this brought the pain and regret freshly to the surface at a time when she was already raw.

She needed to act, do something, take charge of her life. And if she got hurt? Well, right now she couldn't think of anything more agonizing than what she'd already been through.

Was she really ready to date again? More importantly, could she just "date" Rafe Cameron?

Five

The next day, Sarah was itching to give Rafe a swift kick in the butt. After asking her out on a date, insisting they spend the rest of the week together, he'd gone right back to ignoring her again. Not so much as a call.

Hopefully lunch with her best friend would yield some answers to how she should handle him, or at least ease the stress headache building behind her eyes. Margaret Tanner sat across from her at the tiny table on the patio of Bistro by the Sea, a deli/coffee shop in the business district. It kept up a bustling take-out service, but also had a small dining area with tables. Today was definitely a sit-down day, with a breeze coming in off the water and an umbrella on their table to shield them from the sun.

Sarah picked at the parsley alongside her chicken-salad croissant sandwich, her food uneaten but her frazzled nerves gladly soaking up her second mug of coffee.

Margaret set aside her hot grilled panini. "What's wrong? Don't even bother denying it," her friend said with quick confidence. "You may be able to fool the others with that overbright smile, but I know you better."

They'd been years apart in school, but once they were both in their twenties, they'd become friends. There was something about sharing a history with a person and they shared Vista del Mar. Most of all, she appreciated Margaret's unpretentious, no-B.S. manner.

"What tipped you off?" Sarah asked.

"You can barely sit still. You've rearranged the place setting at least three times. And you've checked your cell phone five…make that six times."

She stopped her hand midreach toward her cell resting by the pepper mill. "Oh, I didn't even know."

Margaret flicked back her hair, her look much sleeker these days since her wardrobe makeover when she'd started working for William Tanner. "You still haven't answered my question."

Bells chimed as the door opened, a harried woman in a business suit backing out while holding a huge cup of coffee and a to-go bag. Sarah waited for the woman to pass before answering.

"Rafe's in town." She resisted the urge to snatch up her cell phone, a phone that hadn't rung with a single call from him after their kiss at her place.

"Yeeeees, I noticed that about five months ago."

"I meant, he's back in my life." She tapped her silent phone. "I think."

"So the two of you have finally decided to quit ignoring each other." Margaret grinned, afternoon traffic zipping to and fro behind her.

"Well, it was tough for him not to notice me when I dumped a pitcher of tea in his lap."

"You did what?" Margaret gasped, then laughed.

Sarah waited for the laughter to fade—and waited quite a long time. "I'm surprised you haven't heard since everyone in town has been buzzing—and chuckling—about it. I thought for sure William would have mentioned it."

"We were, uh—" she tugged at her diamond earring stud "—preoccupied when I got home from my business trip last night."

"Preoccupied?" She angled forward, truly happy for her friend. "Wanna dish?"

"You're not going to distract me that easily." Margaret moved the little vase of daisies aside and stared more intently. "We're talking about you and Rafe Cameron getting back together again."

"I wasn't distracting, exactly. I brought it up…." But maybe she had shied away from sharing this at the last second. She didn't exactly have a firm handle on her emotional compass these days. "I wouldn't go so far as to say we're an item, not by a long stretch. But we're talking, trying to end things on a better note than we did fourteen years ago."

"An ending?" Margaret smiled knowingly. "If you two are ending, why are you blushing?"

"It's hot out here." She fanned herself with a menu that stayed on the table.

"Nuh-uh. Can you honestly tell me the spark is gone?" Pausing, her friend blinked fast in surprise. "Oh my God, you're turning redder. Have you two started sleeping together again?"

"Again?" Sarah slapped the menu back on the table in exasperation. "Why does everyone assume we slept together in high school? As crazy as it may seem to you, we did not have sex. We were waiting for marriage."

"Okay, okay, I hear you." Margaret raised her hands in surrender.

Being defensive wouldn't get her anywhere and she genuinely needed advice from someone she could trust. "We're not sleeping together now either."

"But something happened."

"We kissed." Understatement of the year. "And there were definitely sparks." Massive understatement. "Except it can't go anywhere. We had problems fourteen years ago, different priorities and dreams. Those differences have only grown over time."

"And of course when you have irreconcilable differences with a man, the first course of action should be to make out." Margaret bit into her sandwich, almost managing to hide her smirk.

"You're supposed to be on my side here."

"I am." She swiped her mouth with her napkin. "I'm just pointing out what seems obvious to everyone else. You aren't over Rafe, not by a long shot."

"What if it's just sexual frustration?" she asked Margaret, and finally herself as well. "What if I'm just this turned on because I've gone so long without since Quentin died?"

Margaret spluttered halfway through a sip of her sparkling water. "There hasn't been anyone in three years?"

"You know, I'm getting tired of you looking at me like I'm a freak because I don't jump every guy who walks past me."

"And that's my point." Margaret set aside her glass, her eyes astute, dangerously so. "If I'm hearing you right, your husband was your first and only, and you loved him. You haven't slept with another guy since then, regardless of how frustrated you've become. But that could be about to change, with Rafe. Which should tell you something."

That's what scared her most. She'd loved him once and it crushed her when they broke up. Her heart had been shattered again when Quentin died. She couldn't take another blow.

If she knew she could be with Rafe without risk… "He asked me out on a date to Jacques' tonight."

Her friend's eyes flashed with curiosity, followed by concern, solidifying into determination. "Then you're going to need something great to wear…. I know this nifty consignment store with gorgeous designer pieces for a steal." She tossed down two twenties on the table and tugged Sarah's wrist. "Come on, no lollygagging. We need to make a trip to Time Again."

Time Again? God, she hoped it wasn't prophetic, because she didn't intend to march right back into the same old doomed past relationship with Rafe. If she was going to spend time with this man, she refused to have her heart broken again.

Finally, he had Sarah in his car again. One step closer to having her in his bed. He downshifted around a seaside curve on the way to Jacques'.

For work, he drove a 2010 Mercedes-Benz G-Class, roomy enough for his Dream Team or business associates in from out of town. For tonight, however, he drove his Porsche. The finely tuned engine ate up the miles, cars whipping by in flashes of headlights because of his speed rather than theirs. Moonbeams glinted along the dark ocean off to the side.

He had Sarah all to himself for the rest of the week and he would damn well make every second count. He intended to pamper her with everything she deserved, everything he could finally offer her. And hell yeah, he had to admit he got a rush out of having her inside this car that represented how he'd left behind the days of a beat-up El Camino with a busted radio. He'd planned to take her to Jacques' fourteen years ago on Valentine's Day, plans that had fallen through. All he'd been able to offer her was a fistful of flowers and a homemade picnic on the beach. God, she'd stolen his breath that night, heart-stoppingly gorgeous and so damn grateful for too damn little….

Standing on her parents' front porch, Sarah had tipped her head, curls swaying to the side. "What's behind your back?"

Rafe pulled his fist around in front of him, clutching the bouquet of flowers, most of which he didn't even know the names of, but it looked like a burst of color with pinks, yellows, purples and red. It was freaking huge and he probably owed Mr. Rodriguez extra work for all of this. But he wasn't one bit sorry when he saw the way Sarah's eyes lit up.

"Oh Rafe!" she squealed and her feet did an

impromptu tap dance on the wooden porch. She gave him a quick kiss, then gathered up the flowers to her nose, inhaling deeply.

She moaned with a pleasure that made his groin pull tight as he imagined other ways to bring the kittenish sound from her throat. Or maybe it was the kiss that sent his pulse skyrocketing. Either way, he was one uncomfortable dude.

"Oh, Rafe!" she said again with an obvious excitement that couldn't be missed or faked. "These are amazing. I can't believe you did this, and ohmigosh, you are such a good secret-keeper since you didn't even give me a hint all day."

"I'm glad you're happy."

"Very much so." She smiled at him over the flowers, the porch light playing with the hints of gold in her red hair. "Is this what I smelled in your car this morning?"

"You've got me there." He still couldn't believe she'd thought it was the leftover smell of some other girl's perfume.

She scrunched her nose. "I can't believe I was such a jealous brat."

"I would feel the same if I thought you were seeing someone else." Rafe couldn't shake the image of how Quentin Dobbs had looked at her. He knew she wouldn't lie to him, but still. The guy liked her and didn't make any secret of it even though the whole world knew Sarah was dating Rafe.

Possessiveness pumped through his veins. Not smart. He prided himself on being calm, focused.

Sarah put her flowers on the porch swing as carefully

*as she placed an expensive dinner on the table at work.
"I have something for you, too."*

*"You didn't have to do that. I seem to recall someone
with the most amazing red hair and a smoking-hot body
telling me—just this morning—that Valentine's Day is
for girls."*

*She flicked her hair over her shoulders with a sass
that never failed to turn him inside out.*

*"And this girl wanted to get you something." She
reached into her purse and withdrew a small gold gift
bag. "Hope you like it."*

*He plucked through all the tissue paper, decorative
white and clear, both flecked with gold to match the
bag. He and his dad exchanged gifts on Christmas and
birthdays, but they usually passed them over to each
other in the plastic store bag. He hadn't had anything
wrapped up like this since before his mom died.*

*Rafe pushed aside the last of the paper and found…
"A money clip?"*

*Fat lot of use that was going to get. But he smiled
anyway, fast, so as not to hurt her feelings.*

*"It's for all the millions you're going to make." She
pulled the gold money clip from his hands and hooked
it on his tie playfully. "And there's something else in
there, too. Something little and maybe kinda silly, but
I thought you would enjoy it."*

*He stuffed his hand inside, found something small
and metallic. He pulled out…a Matchbox car, a black
Porsche. Now that made him smile for real. She'd
remembered how he talked about dreaming of owning
one and driving it right down Main Street so fast that
Officer Garcia wouldn't even be able to catch him.*

Rafe closed his fingers around the toy car and leaned forward to kiss her, lingering, knowing he should pull back for a bunch of reasons. Number one reason being that Battle-Ax Granny was on the other side of the door. But he'd been thinking about Sarah all day—and it had definitely been a long day that started way too early. So yeah, he wanted to take a few extra seconds to enjoy how soft her lips felt against his, the way she sighed as she kinda melted again his chest.

Her purse thudded to the porch and her sweater slid away. Her fingernails dug into his shoulders in a way he was starting to learn meant she was every bit as into this as he was. He cupped her neck to hold on to not just her, but the kiss a little longer. Fiery red curls brushed against the back of his wrist, softer than anything he could remember feeling. His hands itched to tangle up in her hair, have it all over him. Have her all over him. His blood pounded in his ears, demanding more, more, more.

His hands started shaking from restraint. He needed to cut this short before he lost control right here on her front porch, for crying out loud.

Pulling back, he sketched his fingers down Sarah's creamy smooth cheek. "Thank you. For both gifts. They're great. You're great."

And he really would have been wiser to leave her alone because he didn't have a clue where they could take this relationship once they graduated....

Sarah's purr of happiness pulled Rafe back into the present, his hands on the Porsche's steering wheel, eyes on the road ahead and the most exasperating woman he'd ever known in the passenger seat beside him.

She stroked her fingers along the leather upholstery with another luxurious kitty-cat sigh. "I'm glad you got the Porsche you always dreamed of."

"I'm glad you're finally getting to ride in it."

And he was even more enthused that she remembered how he'd dreamed of owning this vehicle. She hadn't wiped him out of her mind, regardless of how much she held back. Soft oldies piped softly through the sound system, hopefully stirring up a few more of those memories for her.

Sarah turned toward him, her scent drifting with the air conditioner's gusting. "What did you do with yourself all these years you've been gone? Besides make piles and piles of money."

"You haven't been keeping tabs on me?" he teased, keeping his eyes on the winding seaside road, rather than looking at her in that sexy little black number like he wanted. "I'm crushed."

"Yeah, right." She laughed softly. "Your self-esteem looks to be taking a serious hit. Not."

He couldn't afford to doubt himself. Some called him arrogant. He could live with that. So he simply downshifted around a corner without answering.

"Rafe? Care to share what you've been up to?" she prodded again for an answer.

No harm in sharing. "I worked construction in L.A., saved some money—" nearly every cent "—then went to night school to become a C.P.A.—"

"Wait," she interrupted. "Stop right there. You're an accountant?"

Her shock was a little insulting. Not to mention it also let him know she hadn't been searching his name on Google. Sarah had definitely moved on with her life and hadn't given him a second thought.

His hands clenched around the steering wheel. "Yes, I'm an accountant—" He stopped when she started giggling. He glanced over at her pressing a hand to her too perfect chest in the low-cut dress. "What's so funny?"

She swallowed back the laughs, if not her smile. "You never did have much of a sense of humor."

"Then help me out," he said tightly.

"I'm surprised at your major, is all. You just don't seem the accountant type. You're not a pocket-protector-wearing, numbers-crunching kind of guy living in a sparse cubicle."

His ego soothed, he explained, "I learned about money, how to make it and how to make sure no one took it from me. I also got my MBA to broaden my scope, and *voilà*, I became the corporate raider everyone knows and loves today."

"You do have a sense of humor after all." Her laugh came easier this time, stroking his senses across the close confines of the sports car.

"When I need to use it. Most of the time, though, it's just not important to me. I'm not interested in winning popularity contests." He stroked back a loose curl of her hair, testing the silky texture between his fingers. Desire surged through him as strongly as the revving engine. "Just winning. Period."

"Both hands on the wheel, please." She inched her head away but he couldn't miss the way her chest rose and fell faster at his touch. "Now that you've kicked Ronald Worth's corporate butt, what's next?"

He opened his mouth to answer, to divert her from this line of questioning. Far better for them to talk of his plans for Hannah's Hope rather than the dismantling of the outdated factory that produced antiquated microchips for toys and appliances.

A siren cut the night. Then a flashing blue light splashed a reflection in his rearview mirror. Shooting a quick glance at his speedometer, he winced.

Eighty-five. Hell.

It was one thing to open up the engine on a deserted bluff road on his own time, but another entirely to do so with Sarah beside him.

Lifting his foot from the accelerator, he tapped the brakes and eased off to the side of the road. His side mirror showed him an older, but familiar face. Officer Garcia had been a permanent fixture in the high school parking lot back in the day. Reaching for his wallet, he watched the Vista del Mar PD veteran walk toward his car.

Rafe placed his hands on the dashboard and waited.

At least he didn't have to worry about a major confrontation with Officer Garcia. This should go smoothly. He'd recently managed to make friends with the local law enforcement. Officer Garcia had even been pulling some private security shifts for his VIPs. So even though Rafe was grateful for the stop that reminded him to slow down and keep Sarah safe, he also knew there wasn't a chance the guy would give him a hard time anymore when they'd just been shooting the breeze on what

Officer Garcia should do to optimize his retirement fund. Fair or not, that was the way the world worked.

He would slow down the Porsche for sure. But when it came to Sarah? He had no intention of easing off the accelerator.

Six

She'd never been to Jacques' before.

Sarah followed the maître d'—Henri—past the table reputed to be permanently kept open for Rafe and toward the double doors leading outside. They were running about twenty minutes late after Officer Garcia's stop. The police officer may have been more pleasant than when they'd been in high school, but he was still extremely thorough.

At least they didn't have to worry about a reservation being lost or their table being given away. She'd already heard the buzz at her own job about how the place kept a table for Rafe all the time, anytime.

Jacques' was an upscale French seafood restaurant on the beach, even ritzier than the Beach and Tennis Club. Elegant and definitely romantic, with bone china and live music. For a significant sum, Jacques' would set up private tables on the beach.

And tonight, they were definitely dining on the beach.

A gauzy cabana covered their table for two, torches and candles adding to the moonlight's illumination.

Rafe waved Henri away before he could assist Sarah into her chair and reached for it himself. His fingers grazed her shoulders as she took her seat. A violinist played discreetly off to the side.

Sarah tipped her face into the sea breeze carrying lilting notes over her. "Bach. My favorite. How did you know?"

"I phoned Margaret. Your best friend was more than happy to help me out." He held her chair out for her. "Back when we dated, you listened to Garth Brooks and the occasional Spice Girls tune."

"Still do, sometimes." She sat, delicious awareness shimmering through her at his knuckles grazing her back—and that he would care enough to ask her friend about her favorite music now. Then he let go of the seat with a quick glide down her bare arms. She swallowed thickly. "I like classical when I'm working in my garden, and you can wipe the surprised look off your face or I'm going to have to remind you of your own words. Don't make assumptions, right, Mr. Accountant?"

"You have me there." He settled across from her.

Rafe draped a napkin over his knee, looking mouth-wateringly delicious in the charcoal suit. His ice-blue silk tie made his already amazing eyes all the more magnetic. She reached for her glass of sparkling water and sipped too fast, bubbles tickling her nose.

As their waiter arrived to explain the appetizers, Sarah zoned out. Listening to the sharply dressed man list each detail reminded her too much of her own work. When he finished, Sarah simply nodded to Rafe. "You choose since I took care of the last meal."

Not that cheeseburgers had been any great stretch for her.

Thank goodness Margaret had taken her shopping at Time Again so she didn't feel like the poor relation here. She wasn't into appearances, but right now she couldn't help but feel her pride was on the line. A basic little black dress, knee-length, it had a hint of beading along the off-the-shoulder straps. She couldn't miss how his eyes were drawn to her neckline.

Rafe's eye stroked her again—all over—as he lifted his Waterford crystal to toast. "Fourteen years after the fact, but I'm finally making good on my promise to bring you here."

She couldn't deny the place was nice, the service top-notch, but she felt compelled to add, "I enjoyed our Valentine's Day picnic on the beach. And you know you spent much more than you could afford on prom night."

"Hardly. You ate a salad because you were scared of getting mad cow disease."

Something stirred deep inside her, something exciting and scary all at once. "You remember what I ate on prom night?"

"I remember everything about those months we spent dating." His cerulean-blue eyes fell to her bared collarbone again.

"Prom night sure didn't end the way either of us

planned." She still shuddered at the memory of the way the night she'd dreamed about had been cut short.

He scrubbed a hand over his jaw, shaking his head. "I should have known someone would spike the punch."

"You can't be in control of everything."

"Says who?" He angled back as the waiter placed their appetizer on the table, coquilles St. Jacques, sautéed scallops served artfully on a shell.

She shook her head. "People like you have heart attacks and high blood pressure."

"My doctor gave me a hundred percent clean bill of health at my last checkup." He certainly looked at ease in his new world with connections, fancy tastes and high-end clothes that definitely hadn't come from any thrift store.

"Rafe, what are we really doing here?"

"Attracting attention, because you are gorgeous tonight."

"Stop it." She brushed aside his compliment before he could distract her. She knew too well how easily this man could tempt her with his words, his eyes, his *hands*. "I meant, what are we doing by going out? What are we going to accomplish? Even if we sleep together, nothing's going to change."

Gauze from the cabana brushed her chair, floating on the sea breeze.

"If? You obviously underestimate me, Sarah."

She put her water down carefully, anger simmering already. "I'm not some business acquisition to conquer."

"I've always wanted you," he said matter-of-factly even as his eyes blazed hotter than the torches around them. "That hasn't changed. If anything, you're even more stunning now than you were then."

The way he looked at her stirred her too-long-neglected needs. Why could he tempt her in ways no one else had? "You broke my heart once. You'll forgive me if I'm not so quick to let you do it again."

"Maybe you'll break my heart."

She rolled her eyes, refusing to be swayed by his skillful maneuverings any more than the romantic candlelight and distant crashing waves. "Rumor around here is that you don't have one anymore."

He took her hand and placed her fingers across his wrist, above the cotton of his tailored shirt cuff, just along his racing pulse. "I most certainly do still have a heart in working order and it's beating double time because of how damn much I want you."

What a crazy desire to want to believe his racing heart meant more than that. "Sex and love are two different things."

"That's not what you said back when we were dating, when you wanted to wait until we were married. So, Sarah, is my heart racing because I love you? Or are sex and love different?" His pulse slugged harder against her fingers with every word.

Her mouth went so dry she couldn't have answered even if she wanted to, and she most definitely was not ready to venture into any scary emotional waters with Rafe. But she couldn't bring herself to tell him to stop either.

When she didn't speak, he continued, his voice husky, "In which case we can finally be together all night long in every position imaginable while still keeping our hearts in check."

Snatching her hand away, she slumped back in her chair, fingers twisting in her lap to numb away the feel of his hot skin and throbbing response. "I can see now why you're such a successful businessman. You sure do know how to present your case."

"You didn't answer my question."

"That's my prerogative."

Could she just sleep with Rafe without her feelings becoming entangled? Margaret's caution from earlier rolled around inside her head.

She didn't think she could stay that detached. Which meant she either had to walk away, leave the table and the date this instant, or she would have to get to know the adult Rafe better in order to make a decision she could be at peace with for the rest of her life. She was older now, wiser, no longer the wide-eyed, impetuous teenager. She could tread warily, but with determination.

Maybe there was something to this attraction, something beneath the hunger that hadn't faded in all those years.

Still scared as hell, she made her decision. "Well, then, let's get started with dinner. Because I'm famished."

"I take that to mean you're ready?"

Nerves bubbled in her stomach faster than the fizzing sparkling water on the table. "I do believe I am."

The restaurant lights dimmed behind them as Jacques' finished up its final seating for the night.

Rafe studied Sarah through the amber liquid of his vintage port, facets cut into the crystal multiplying her image enticingly. She sipped her sherry, the meal over, his promise to take her to Jacques' finally complete fourteen years after the fact.

Or almost complete.

He wasn't quite ready to say good-night to Sarah yet and the wait staff would linger for as long as Rafe remained. Setting aside his drink, he stood abruptly. Was that a flash of disappointment in her jade-green eyes?

Good.

"Walk with me on the beach," he demanded.

A smile twitched at the corners of her lush lips. "I don't much like your dictatorial tone."

He extended his hand anyway.

"Rafe, we'll just be talking."

Again, he didn't bother answering. They argued too much and he wanted to touch her, to find that connection with her that was buried beneath her worries about the Worth plant…now Cameron Enterprises, if only she could admit that.

Sighing, she linked her fingers with his. "God, you are infuriating and I really should just go home."

"But you're going to come with me anyway."

He locked his fingers around hers, enjoying the feel of her soft skin against his, just like he remembered. Near the end of their relationship, she'd put those hands all over him, even bringing him to completion more than once. In his car, here on the beach, up in her bedroom when he snuck through the window…

His body tightened in response to just the memory

and her hand in his as they cleared the walkway down a bluff to the shoreline. Keeping himself in check, especially with the ocean breeze whipping the hem of her dress over his legs, was going to be damn tough.

Sarah leaned to slip off her shoes. "Tell me about the women in your life."

What the hell? "No."

"Excuse me?" She straightened, high heels dangling from her fingers by the straps.

"I said, 'No.'" And he meant it. "That's not a conversation I wish to have with you."

"Why not?"

"You're asking so you can get riled up and put distance between us. All that matters is that I'm not seeing anyone now. Except you." He tipped her chin with his knuckle. "Believe me, you have my complete and undivided attention."

She swayed toward him for an instant before easing away. "That's not exactly true. You're still completely focused on your vendetta against Ronald Worth."

"Hmm…. That I am." He plucked her shoes from her fingers and tossed them by the path as they'd done so often as teens. "Yet, you're still here with me tonight."

"To persuade you."

He pulled off his leather shoes that had cost more than his first car. "What does that have to do with women I may have dated?" He dropped his shoes and socks by her heels. "Nothing, of course. But thank you for being jealous."

She spluttered, backing along the beach. "I am not jealous. Just, uhm, curious."

"And blushing. I can see it even in the moonlight."

He followed her, tracking her step for step. "Do you still blush all the way down to your breasts?"

"Argh, you are such a…"

"A man."

Laughing, she sprinted away. The wind whipped her hair around her in a fan as she raced toward the water. A wave lapped at her feet and she squealed, moving back a step. Gathering the hem of her flowy skirt in her fist, she stepped into the surf. Splashing. Dancing.

Enchanting him.

There was something so uninhibited about the way she lived in the moment, whether she was stepping in the surf with both feet or letting loose on him in a public restaurant, putting her job on the line to speak her mind. And as much as he'd wished she could be more practical, plan for the future, he also couldn't look away. At least Jacques' was nothing more than distant lights now and no one else could see the sensual magnificence in front of him.

The edges of her dress soaked up water, not that she seemed to care. Moonlight danced just as fast along the curve of her face tipped up in abandon. He was so damn mesmerized and turned on he could have sworn the sand shifted under his feet.

A waved slapped her, plastering her dress to her body. She'd been his every teenage fantasy back in the day, and now she was even more lushly his present-day craving. Without another thought, he waded in after her.

"Rafe," she gasped, "what are you doing? You'll wreck your suit."

"You've ruined your dress."

"But you don't shop at thrift stores."

He wanted to tell her she didn't have to pinch pennies anymore, but he knew from experience that would kill the mood fast. So he simply scooped her up into his arms, damp and warm and so very soft against his chest.

With the slam of the next wave, his mouth met hers. Her arms looped around his neck without hesitation, her lips parting, accepting, tasting. Her breasts pressed more fully against his chest until he could swear he felt the tightening buds against him. Felt his own response in spite of the ocean soaking his ankles.

Turning back to shore, he kept her against him, tasting and exploring this woman who was so familiar and new all at once.

When his feet hit dry sand again, he eased her to her feet. Her wet body sealed to his, her fingers threading through his hair as she gave back kiss for kiss, moan for moan. He went even harder pressed to the sweet warmth of her stomach. She wriggled nearer, launching a fresh burst of need through his veins.

His hands slid lower to cup under her bottom and lift her off her feet. One step at a time, he backed her toward a nearby bluff. Close, but not nearly close enough in his estimation.

Once he could be sure they were completely shielded from the rest of the world, he eased her toes back to the sand again. As she nipped at his ear, he shrugged out of his jacket and tossed it on the ground. He lowered her onto his coat and stretched out over her.

She bunched his shirt up and up, her fingers scratching along his back with a frenzy he couldn't miss. He sketched kisses down her neck, to her shoulder, nuzzling aside the shoulder of her dress, baring the top of one sweet, full breast. The moonlight bathed the creamy mound perfectly for his eyes and he looked his fill before taking her in his mouth. Teasing lightly with his tongue, his teeth, tucking his hand inside to explore more of her.

Wind rolled in off the water, but not nearly enough to cool the sweat popping along his brow and his back. Grit carried in the breeze, bringing a realization that he was seconds away from pulling down her panties right here and now. That somehow he had less self-control with Sarah now than at eighteen.

He buried his face in her neck. "We can't do this here."

She grabbed two fistfuls of his hair and tugged his head up until he stared into her eyes. "Why the hell not?"

Her needy wriggle sent a fresh bolt of desire straight to his already aching groin.

"Because we're on the damn beach, lying on my jacket. Let's at least shuffle to my place." He rested his forehead against hers. "I'll shower you in roses and eat strawberries off your body. We'll drink champagne in the hot tub. I'll give you all the romance I couldn't afford back then."

She stilled completely under him, giving him only a second's warning before she shoved at his shoulders. "You haven't changed at all."

"I'm not sure I follow." He rolled to his side, studying her face pulled tight and angry in the moonlight.

"It's still all about the money to you." She scraped up

the shoulders on her dress. "What things you can give me. Right here, right now, I only wanted you."

He heard the honesty in her words and realized what he'd almost tossed away. He cupped her waist and skimmed his mouth over her brow, inhaling the floral scent of her shampoo. "Okay then, that's what we'll do. We'll stay here."

She scooted aside and sat up abruptly. "No, thank you. The mood has definitely been broken. I'd like to go home. Now, please."

Her sure anger took the temperature down about twenty degrees. She wasn't joking. His window of opportunity had closed for the night because he'd let his words get ahead of his brain. He knew better, damn it. He understood utterly and completely that he had to tread warily when it came to Sarah and money. But she'd honest-to-God seemed to enjoy herself this evening and he'd lost his edge.

He'd been a reckless dumb ass, something that never happened.

Except around Sarah. He shoved to his feet and extended his hand. Thank God he had enough of his brain in working order to let go and walk silently beside her. With each step back to their shoes and into his Porsche, he reminded himself he still had the rest of the week to make another opportunity, and that chance was more likely to roll around if he eased off tonight.

The drive back to her place was quieter, with none of the excitement and anticipation of their ride to the restaurant. Sarah stared out the window. Her hair shielded her face in an impenetrable red curtain until he didn't have a clue what she thought.

So he kept his eyes forward. No need to risk a ticket from Officer Garcia two times in one night.

He drove by the tiny houses in Sarah's neighborhood. She didn't live in the best section of town by any stretch, but the place seemed all the more run-down in the shadowy darkness. Certainly none of them were as well-tended as her freshly painted place with its perfect little lawn. He clenched his jaw, resisting the temptation to offer a legion of help creating her tropical works of art without her dirtying her hands.

Turning into her driveway, he pulled up behind her econo car parked under the carport. She reached for her door handle.

He shot her a look. "Don't even think about it. It doesn't cost me a thing to walk you to your porch."

Before she could argue, he stepped outside—and stopped short.

Her front door stood open, the glass panel shattered. Protectiveness surged through him, along with a mind-numbing fear that something could have happened to her. That she would have been alone and vulnerable in there. That he could have lost her in a way far more permanent than any breakup.

Bile scoured his gut. His instincts about this neighborhood had been dead-on, damn it. He would be talking to the Vista del Mar police again tonight after all.

And to hell with Sarah's prickly pride. He would be taking her home with him tonight.

Seven

"I am *not* going to your place, Rafe," Sarah insisted, sweeping the glass into a dustpan as the police cruiser drove away.

The neighborhood was quiet now, all the initial gawkers returning to their homes to sleep. Where had they been when someone was breaking into her home? Why hadn't somebody stepped up and stopped it, or at least called the cops? Only streetlights and dim stars lit the road this late, nearly one in the morning.

She might be outwardly calm, but inside she was shaking to think that some criminal had broken into her home and pawed through her things. "Don't even bother trying to convince me."

"I didn't ask." He set the trash can down in front of her, his shirtsleeves rolled up, his tie loosened.

His face was impassive, deceptively so. She could

see too well the flexing of his jaw, the pulse throbbing in his temple in time with the night bugs buzzing—Jerusalem crickets, they were called. Out of the blue she remembered Rafe telling her the name of those creatures long ago. So much of Rafe was knit into the fiber of her past.

"But you were going to." She dumped the glass from the busted-out door window into the bin. Her skin itched from tension—and the gritty sand and dried salt water from their crazy make-out session on the beach. Unfulfilled need tightened and ached between her thighs.

"Hypothetically speaking," he said, leaning against the doorjamb, "it would be wrong for me to ask you to come home with me because…?"

Because she wouldn't be able to resist tearing his clothes off and working through the tension in her body the good old-fashioned way. Having sex with Rafe because she was scared offered a recipe for morning-after regrets.

"If you want to be helpful, put those rusty carpenter skills of yours to work and nail a board over that gaping hole in my front entrance." God, she really wished she had a big dog right now, one with a massive bark.

Rather like Rafe.

"Do you really think a piece of plywood will keep a criminal out?" He eyed her neighborhood with a skepticism that raised her hackles.

"Officer Garcia said they already caught the guys who did this." While Garcia had been filling out the report, a call had come in about two teenage males breaking into another house three streets over. "The petty thieves didn't even get much for their efforts, just an iPod and some costume jewelry, which I will get back as soon as the case is cleared."

"It was too easy for them to get in here, it wasn't all that late and no one noticed." His eyes grew blue-flame hotter, angrier with each word. "What do you think they would have done if you'd been home? If you'd been in bed or in the shower?"

His hands fisted at his sides, corded muscles bunched and jumped under the fine cotton of his dress shirt. The intensity in his voice, in his very being went beyond the corporate shark who took down anyone in his path. This was Rafe, the man at his most elemental, prepared to stand immovable between her and anything that came near her.

He'd done so in the past, when they'd been teens. An unruly spring breaker had propositioned her, pinching her thigh hard enough to leave a bruise. Once Rafe saw it, he hadn't let up until he found the guy and pummeled the hell out of him. He'd been lucky the rich kid's dad hadn't pressed charges.

Part of her wanted to caution him, and the other part couldn't deny she was drawn to his strength, to his charisma, to having someone to stand by her and help carry the weight of a life that could be so very hard and unfair. As much as she hated to admit it, the thought of staying here did frighten her. She'd been by herself for three years, but tonight, she felt truly alone and vulnerable for the first time.

Stepping deeper into her house, Rafe continued, "Tomorrow morning, I'll have new locks and a top-of-the-line security system installed." He held up a bold, broad palm. "Don't even bother commenting on my materialism. This is about your safety. It's late. Stay with me tonight. We can talk more over breakfast."

His Gucci loafers looked so incongruous on her simple braid rug.

She should tell him she would call her parents or her grandmother and stay with them. But it was so very late…and she wanted to be with Rafe, no matter how unwise.

"Okay, you win." Sarah nodded slowly. "But I still want you to cover the door."

"I'll take care of it while you pack an overnight bag."

The private elevator dinged through three levels as they neared the top floor to Rafe's condo. He stood beside her silently. His pants had dried, a little wrinkled along the hem by their impromptu ocean frolic. But otherwise, he looked as perfectly pressed as when he'd picked her up hours earlier.

She, on the other hand, had changed from her dress into jeans, a peasant top and flip-flops before packing her bag. Her pink floral overnight bag looked so incongruous in Rafe's grasp, but he insisted on carrying her "luggage."

She hadn't seen the inside of his beach place, but she knew units in this part of Vista del Mar went for top dollar and his was reputed to have cost over three million. How much money, how many things, would Rafe amass before he realized it wasn't going to bring him happiness?

Frustration and sympathy warred inside her. But

then Rafe had always stirred a mix of emotions. Yet, here she was with him, convincing herself she'd chosen to come to his place because she didn't want to disrupt her parents and grandmother after midnight. Even though a tiny, annoying voice in the back of her head reminded her that her parents were night owls after working the late shift for years. And there had to be at least a dozen other people she could have called, including her friend Margaret.

But she hadn't.

The elevator doors slid open and Rafe waved her inside. The space was long and airy, with a bachelor-esque Mediterranean style consisting of tall plants, terra-cotta floors and wrought iron accessories. A dining room led into a living area. White walls and tall windows provided a unifying theme, while the furniture was a rich polished wood, with tan leather and cream upholstery. An incredible view waited beyond the glass doors leading to a to-die-for balcony.

She slid off her shoes by habit and tucked them by the elevator. The planked ceiling gave the impression of an upside-down ark as she walked deeper inside, stone tiles cool beneath her feet.

The place was a showpiece, no question. And starkly impersonal. Like Rafe, right now.

He draped his jacket over the back of the cream sofa in front of the fireplace. "You'll sleep in my room. Alone, of course."

Brusquely, he led her down the connecting hall. Where was the man who'd wined and dined her earlier with sensual promise and intensity?

"That's generous, but not necessary." She paused by what appeared to be a door to a spare room.

"I have work to take care of. The spare room is being used as an office. There's a substantial sofa in there when I'm finished."

Pushing open the door at the end of the corridor, he revealed a king-size bed with a mahogany platform and a plump white duvet, stacked high with tan and brown pillows.

A wide bed made for uninhibited, roll-around-the-mattress sex.

Rafe placed her bag on a burgundy leather chair by the sliding doors, the roar of the Pacific calling just beyond the glass. He padded back across the room toward her with pantherlike stealth. She remembered that quiet but focused walk well. He'd carried that trademark intensity even as a teen, merely honing it over the years.

He stalked closer. Nerves tingled to life, nerves that had nothing to do with fear and everything to do with excitement, anticipation. Passion. Her toes curled against the floor as she waited for his next move.

Was he going to kiss her good-night? Would he push again for more? He reached toward her and she waited. Wanted.

His hand extended past her and flicked on the electric fireplace, flames low and soothing. He backed out of the door, his voice drifting through as he pulled it closed after him. "Dream of me, Sarah."

Damn. Her knees folded and thank goodness the edge of the mattress caught her or she would have been sitting in the middle of the floor like an idiot. She chided herself for her quick slide into a sensual haze just from being here in his home, surrounded by his things and his scent. What business did she have thinking about rolling around in Rafe's bed with him? She forced her legs to steady and walked to her tiny little overnight duffel.

Searching through her pink floral bag for her nightshirt, she couldn't help feeling strangely aware of taking her clothes off in Rafe's home. In his bedroom.

What had come over her tonight? Lingering in the open sliding glass doors to stare out at the stormy ocean sky, she thought about how fast she'd been ready to give in to what they both wanted on the beach earlier. She didn't know how much longer she could hold out, even with reminders of why she shouldn't leap right back into his arms.

She squeezed her eyes closed against the ache building between her legs. If she could just sleep, maybe she would have more self-control, more reason, in the morning. She turned away from the window and the view that called to mind too many times testing her sensual boundaries with Rafe.

Carefully, she folded the plump duvet across the end of the bed, then clicked off the lights. Sliding between the Egyptian-cotton sheets, she rested her cheek on her hands with an exhausted sigh—and found little relief as his scent wrapped more firmly around her, calling to mind his parting words. *"Dream of me, Sarah."*

And she did….

Sarah grabbed Rafe's wrist and pulled his hand out from under her tank top. Having him sneak into her bedroom while her parents slept offered the incredible chance to be alone. But might well offer more temptation than she could withstand.

"Enough," she gasped, flopping onto her back on her bed. Her comforter had long ago been kicked to the floor as they rolled around making out. "If we keep going, I'm not sure if I could stop, and I'm just not ready. Okay?"

Breathing heavily, he rolled onto his side, toying with her hair, his eyes lingering on her chest. Where he'd been touching her two seconds ago. Driving her absolutely crazy. She pressed her legs together against the ache that built more and more every time she was with Rafe.

"Okay, Sarah, your call." He still played with a lock of her hair, but otherwise kept his hands to himself.

She knew that had to be costing him. She'd felt just how bad he wanted her. "We'll have to make sure we're at a really public beach tomorrow so we don't get too tempted."

His eyes slid away from hers again, this time scanning the rock posters on her wall. "Someday I'm going to give you a real vacation. I'll take you to the best concerts in the biggest cities. How about London?"

"I'm happy with a day at the beach. And who wants to waste all our time together traveling? What's wrong with a simple drive to San Diego?"

"I offer you England and you want somewhere we've seen before?" He tugged her hair lightly. "Where's your sense of adventure?"

She nudged his bare foot with hers. "You're about as much adventure as I can take."

"Okay, let's try this again. If you could plan a vacation anywhere—" he rushed to add *"—anywhere other than California, where would it be?"*

She thought hard. That kind of life seemed so far in the future, but if playing the what-if game would make Rafe happy, then okay. "I would want someplace where we could be alone, just the two of us. No interruptions."

Totally committed. Totally married. But she kept that part of the dream to herself for now.

Thank God he hadn't seen the inside of her history notebook when he'd shuffled her project around since she'd practiced writing Mrs. Rafe Cameron about a hundred and fifty times during class.

He tucked her closer. "Alone together sounds good. Continue."

Snuggling against his side, she listened to his heartbeat and inhaled the clean soapy scent on his neck. "No work or obligations. But it would still need to feel homey. I wouldn't want some generic hotel room."

"So you want to own a vacation home." His knuckles skimmed along her back, up and down her spine deliciously. "Where would you like to build it?"

"A vacation home?" She wouldn't have to move, and she wouldn't be stuck in some stark hotel. "Yes, I guess that would work."

"Everything would be there for you so you wouldn't even need to pack. Now, where?" he asked again.

"If a person's going to have a vacation house, then it should be somewhere different than where you live every day. I can go to the beach anytime. Somewhere

cooler maybe." She blew against his neck lightly. "The mountains, I think. A ski cabin with a pond."

"Keep going." He dug his head back into the pillow.

"Nevada." She plucked the state out of the sky at random, somewhere not too far away. "A woodsy, homey cabin that has high ceilings with big fat beams and windows that take up an entire wall."

"Consider it yours."

"You're so funny." She arched up to kiss his jaw. "Really, though, I really just want more time with you. And if you're working eighteen-hour days to buy us stuff, then what's the use? We won't get to enjoy them together."

He stayed quiet, their old money-versus-simple-pleasures argument sort of bouncing around in the air between them like a beach ball just out of reach....

Sarah bolted upright, blinking back confusion as she looked around the unfamiliar bedroom—Rafe's room in his beachside condominium. Their dinner, the break-in, driving here—the whole crazy evening came rushing back, tangling up with her dream still close to the surface.

More than a dream, really. It had been a memory of another time when she and Rafe had been close. That night with him had come back in such perfect clarity that she could still feel his hands on her oversensitive skin.

She clutched the Egyptian-cotton sheets to her chest, the fireplace crackling lowly, just enough to soothe and offer light, but not so much as to overheat the room on a summer night. An ocean wind blew in through the open balcony door, heavy with the humidity of an incoming storm. As much as she vowed she didn't care about money, she couldn't deny enjoying the extravagance of an ocean view.

The crisp breeze caressed her arms and legs, left bare by her overlong nightshirt. She had nicer nightclothes, but she'd defiantly tossed in her favorite, threadbare and sporting a beach festival logo. She hugged her arms tighter around her breasts, which were pebbling from the night air….

Hell, who was she kidding? Her body responded to just the thought of Rafe. Everything she'd felt for him, the intense ache to be with him, seemed so real right now she could have been that lovesick eighteen-year-old. Over the years since he'd left town, she'd almost convinced herself it was just a crush. Inexperience and hormones must have accounted for the attraction, the supreme sexual frustration.

But after the kisses they'd exchanged in the past couple of days, she knew better. They shared a unique, explosive draw to each other and time hadn't dulled it one bit. Rafe had made the first move toward finally exploring those feelings.

Now the next move was up to her.

Rafe needed to get up and move around.

But he couldn't blame too much time in front of the computer for the restlessness stirring inside him. His tension, his frustration had everything to do with Sarah.

With one finger, he rolled a Matchbox Porsche back

and forth along the teak table that doubled as a desk in his spare bedroom. The sheen had long left the black paint, but the little toy was fourteen years old, after all, and he'd taken it out more than a few times.

Keeping it had been ridiculous, sentimental and not at all like him. But he never could bring himself to toss it away. After a while, it had become his good-luck charm. Right now, it was a reminder of how much she'd meant to him.

Too much.

Lightning split the sky out over the ocean, painting a white streak right down the middle of the Pacific. Seconds later, thunder rumbled. The night was heavy with humidity and unanswered questions.

Having her here under his roof should make him happy. Instead, he was edgy, thinking about her home being vandalized. A shower and change into jeans and a T-shirt hadn't done much for loosening the kinks in his neck.

He turned away from the murky ocean beyond his open balcony door and back to the tiny race car. They'd started dating because he'd seen her walking to a bus stop late after work one night. Concern for her safety had propelled him to pick her up after her shift the next night. He hadn't intended to date her—there hadn't been enough money or time for a girlfriend. But once she'd slid inside his car and the rest of the way under his skin, they'd started a five-month relationship that left its mark on him still.

So why was he so damn edgy?

"Rafe?" Sarah called softly from his memory…and from across the room.

He turned the chair to find her standing in the open balcony door. His fist closed around the toy car until metal cut into his palm. Sarah was here. With him. Like a reverse echo of the past, she'd come into his room.

Lightning cut a jagged swath in the distance, adding a crackle to the air. Or maybe it wasn't the weather. Maybe it was her.

She wore a loose, thin T-shirt that stopped just above her knees. Her long legs seemed to stretch forever, calling to his hands to explore every inch the way he'd done when they were dating.

And her breasts.

If he let himself take in the fullness, imagine cradling the weight in his hands, he would have her on the sofa and underneath him in a heartbeat.

He tucked the toy car under a folder and stayed seated, stretching his legs in front of him. "Having trouble sleeping?"

Sarah shrugged, the gentle movement of her breasts under her nightshirt making him throb in response. Yes, he definitely would be gluing himself to this seat. He gripped the arms of the chair for good measure. Better there than on her hips.

"Maybe the incoming storm has me on edge. It's been an eventful night." She scratched the top of her bare foot with her toes. "Your place is lovely."

The nightshirt hitched on her thigh and his gaze tracked the movement. Hell, he could keep his limbs under control but he made no promises about where his eyes went. Not when she wore so little it made even his teeth hurt.

"But it's not at all to your taste." A wry smile tugged at his mouth.

"Why would you say that?" Wind played with her loose hair the way he had earlier tonight.

"It's showy, impersonal—" he raised a finger with each point "—no yard to speak of, not a small-town family place."

"Is that why you chose it? As some sort of statement? Because it was the opposite of everything you grew up with?"

He'd bought it because he thought his mother would have liked the view. But thoughts of his mother's death scratched too close to the surface tonight, especially after the break-in at Sarah's. He couldn't stop envisioning what could have happened if she'd gone home alone, walked in on the burglar....

He scratched over the knot gathering in his chest. "It was on the market and it was flashy. I needed to make a point fast that I am in control." He held up his tumbler of spring water and clinked the ice. "Would you like a drink?"

"We both know I can't hold my alcohol." She eyed his glass with a frown and he didn't bother clearing up her misconception that he was sitting around getting wasted. He wasn't drunk.

"You were eighteen and a very good girl, so you had no reason to have a tolerance for spiked prom punch."

"I still can't drink blue fruit punch to this day. The wine at dinner was plenty for me." She stepped deeper inside, leaning a hip against his desk. "What are you doing?"

He eyed her warily. If he didn't know better, he would think she was trying to seduce him.

Maybe he would need to get wasted after all to survive this conversation. "Reviewing some paperwork for Hannah's Hope. New ways to increase the initial investment so we can take on larger projects."

"You made quite an impression with the launch party last month." She hitched a hip higher to sit on the edge of the teak table. "Your mother would be proud."

"I can't take credit. My event planner—Paige Adams— organized the shindig."

"That's right." She trailed a finger down a polished brass banker's lamp, her foot swinging. "You have a staff now. I'm happy for you, you know, that you have everything you've ever wanted."

His eyes followed her stroke down the antique lamp and he imagined the same sure caress on his skin. "Not everything."

"There were some, uh, loose ends to our relationship." Her toe grazed his leg. He jolted. At first he thought the contact was accidental, but then her eyes turned a deeper green he remembered well. But there, the similarity to the younger Sarah ended.

Lightning and thunder cracked closer together this time. The storm was nearer. The air was thicker. This woman wasn't the inexperienced teen, unsure of committing to the moment. Sarah grazed her foot up his calf with all the confident seduction of a woman who knew what she wanted.

And her eyes said she wanted him.

Eight

She was going to do this. Finally, she was going to sleep with Rafe. She pushed aside all the questions that Margaret had raised earlier. This wasn't about her heart, damn it. This was about a gnawing sexual ache and an insatiable need to know the answer to a question that had plagued her for years.

Would sex with Rafe be as amazing as she'd dreamed?

She inched her toes up the back of his calf, stopping at his knee.

Growling possessively, he shot to his feet. He hooked his hands on her hips and stepped between her thighs. Her fingers twisted in the warm cotton of his T-shirt and she yanked him closer. He kissed her, hard and fiercely and she met him with every bit as much intensity.

Electricity shimmered along her skin as if she'd touched one of those lightning bolts splicing the night sky, and she couldn't just tell herself it was due to abstinence. This was about Rafe.

Firmly, he guided her closer and her legs locked around his waist in a gasping heartbeat. He was warm and hard against her core. Her T-shirt hitched upward and he palmed her thighs.

She moaned into his mouth.

"Hurry," she whispered.

"We'll get there, Kitten." His lips slid over to her ear, down her neck as he whispered gravelly words of encouragement. His urgent tone registered more than his words.

Rocking against him, she scored her fingers down his back, nipped at his ear. Raw desire clawed her insides and she couldn't hold back a whimper.

Rafe angled away, his blue eyes ardent. "Am I hurting you? Are you sure about this?"

"You're not hurting me and God, yes, I'm absolutely certain."

"I don't know what changed your mind, but I'm damn glad we're on the same page." He slipped his hands under her bottom and lifted her from the desk. "Let's go to my room."

She clutched his shoulders more fiercely. "I don't want to wait for you to line the room with gold and rose petals and whatever other trappings you think I need. I want you here. Now."

"Whatever you want."

She *wanted* closure. No more being tormented by dreams of Rafe. She had to put the unresolved feelings to rest so she could finally move on with her life.

Raindrops began a slow patter along the balcony as he carried her to the sofa, easing her down and reclining on top of her in one smooth move. The wealthy texture of the supple leather under her couldn't be missed.

All the same, something about the moment reminded her of making out in his El Camino. A narrow seat. Waves crashing in the background. Denim and cotton. She could almost persuade herself they were teens again, wildly in love with a wide open future.

They'd done everything but go all the way back then, using their hands and mouths to pleasure each other in those last frantic weeks together. When she'd prayed he would change his mind and stay rather than move to L.A. with Bob and Penny.

But she didn't want to think of that time. She wanted to exist in the here and the now. If she let her mind linger overlong on the past, she feared she would realize just how significant this moment was.

She bunched his T-shirt in her fists as he tugged her nightshirt. Her well-worn cotton flew through the air and landed on top of his. Then…sigh…warm flesh met warm flesh, her breasts against his chest. Desire thickened her blood, her pulse slugging heavily in her ears. She fumbled with the fly on his jeans, her hands shaking with need.

Rafe cradled her face. "We have all night."

"Good." She eased his zipper down. "Then we can do this again."

"Excellent point." He levered off her and reached for his wallet resting on the desk. The open fly offered a tempting view of tanned skin and dark blond hair that her eyes followed lower....

His gaze held hers, heating in response to her stare. "Hold that thought. I just need a second to get a condom."

A condom. Of course.

Biting her lip, she swallowed back the tears that threatened to steal the mood. The chances of her getting pregnant were slim, but she couldn't talk about that with him, especially not now. So she stayed silent.

Then he slid his jeans down and off. She couldn't have formed words even if she tried. He stood naked and bronzed in the full light of the room, moonlight behind him. The tumultuous sky backdrop seemed appropriate somehow. The rain picked up speed, the storm building force overhead.

Much like the storm inside her begging to be unleashed.

Her eyes drank him in like the ground soaking up moisture after a long parched dry spell. His body was more muscled, more mature. He'd been a turn-on before, but now? He was everything.

He slid both hands along her hips, hooking his fingers into her panties and easing them down, down, down her legs, off and flinging them away. She opened her arms for him, drawing him on top of her.

His head fell to her breasts, his hands and his tongue teasing and pleasing until she forgot all about doubts or fears, the disappointments of lost babies, lost dreams. He remembered well just how she liked to be touched. And she recalled just how he liked to be stroked, caressed, cradled in her palm. They'd learned together and there was something special about being with someone who understood her wants on such an instinctive level.

Kissing his way back up her chest and along her neck, he captured her mouth again. Anticipation ramping, she hooked her legs higher over his hips. She guided him closer, opening wider to welcome him until finally...

He pressed into her, thickly, slowly, until every nerve throbbed to life. The intensity of it all—sensations emotions, inevitability—rolled over her. Her heels dug deeper into his flanks to urge him closer, her head thrashing as she rolled her hips for... "More...!"

She didn't even realize she'd spoken until he smiled against her mouth with masculine confidence and thrust deeper.

Pleasure rippled through her, then again as he moved inside her. His eyes held hers as he watched her. Somehow it seemed perfect that they should gaze at each other, share this moment as intimately as possible. They'd both certainly waited long enough to be together.

Her fingers roved his back, his hands just as busy as if he would love her with every part of his body. The scent of his aftershave and building perspiration mingled with the earthy smell of leather.

The wildness in his blue stare built and he became more and more *her* Rafe, the Rafe she'd known and loved. He'd been her ever-brooding intense fantasy back then, rather than the detached man, the cold corporate mogul who'd come back to Vista del Mar. All the feelings of fourteen years ago spiraled through her in synch with the roll of her hips against his. She had him in her arms and the rightness of it all brought tears to her eyes.

Release pounded through her suddenly, catching her by surprise then sweeping her away. The roaring in her ears echoed the crashing Pacific waves hammering the shore. Rafe moved faster inside her, drawing out the pleasure, wringing another orgasm and another until her body sagged limply back.

As he buried his face in her neck, she gathered him closer. His body was slick against hers and heavy, but she didn't want to let go. Not yet.

She wasn't sure how long they lay wrapped around each other, linked in the moment and by the perspiration sealing their bodies. But she did know one thing.

She had her answer to a question that had plagued her for fourteen years. Sex with Rafe was every bit as perfect as she'd thought it would be.

But was he the same in every other way, including the ones that had torn them apart before?

Her hands skimmed the muscled planes of his broad back. If only she could be sure she wasn't risking heartache all over again.

Sarah slid sideways past a packed table at the Vista del Mar Beach and Tennis Club, carefully balancing the two lunch orders. By the window, Ana Rodriquez sat with journalist Gillian Preston. From what she'd overheard earlier, apparently they were working on publicity for Hannah's Hope's latest project—expanding multilingual offerings at the library.

There was no escaping reminders of Rafe, even here at work.

Her body still tingled with the memory of making love to him. Never had she watched the clock so closely, wishing away the seconds until her shift ended. If only she could ignore the niggling voice in the back of her mind insisting this was just too good to be true.

Carefully, she placed the heavy load on the wooden tray stand. She checked her notes to see who'd ordered what, the women's conversation washing over her.

Gillian Preston placed her water glass on the table. "I wondered if Hannah's Hope was just a scam for Rafe to hide funny dealings in Cameron Enterprises. But I have to confess, Ana, I'm pleasantly surprised at all the good works coming out of the foundation."

"Me too," Ana answered, her engagement ring catching the sunlight streaming through the wall of windows overlooking the ocean. "I have to pinch myself every day to make sure I'm not imagining it. Heading up Hannah's Hope is a dream job. And I can reassure you from the inside, this charity is the real deal—"

Uncomfortable eavesdropping, and even more uncomfortable with the notion of getting caught listening in, Sarah cleared her throat to gain their attention.

"Gillian, here's your Caribbean vegetable soup." She placed the fragrant steaming bowl in front of the newly married journalist. "And Ana, here's your spinach and prosciutto salad. Be sure to save room for dessert. We just added a pomegranate sorbet that is to die for."

Ana touched the empty chair beside her. "Is there

any chance you could take your break and join us for some of that sorbet?"

Toasting with her water glass, Gillian added, "Or something deeply, decadently chocolate?"

Laughing lightly, Sarah gripped the back of the chair. "Wish I could, but I just clocked in. And my boss still hasn't quite gotten over how I dumped a whole pitcher in Rafe's lap."

A smile dug dimples into Ana's face. "So that isn't a rumor? It really happened?"

Sarah rolled her eyes. "Not one of my finer moments."

Gillian toyed with her fork. "I hear from Max that the two of you and Rafe are mending fences."

"Hmm…" Sarah answered noncommittally, not so sure she wanted their relationship out there just yet. "We're talking without throwing things."

Ana covered her hand and squeezed. "I'm glad to hear it. The way you two looked at each other back in high school was something special. And seeing firsthand all the good work he's doing with Hannah's Hope makes me optimistic he will figure something out to save the factory as well."

A chill settled in Sarah's gut. So easily she'd let herself become distracted from the most important reason for spending time with Rafe. She should have been working to persuade him not to shutter the plant and put most of Vista del Mar out of work. How could she have so easily forgotten what a corporate raider Rafe had become over the years?

Even with her heart in danger, more than ever, she

needed to spend time with Rafe and pray she could bring him around to her way of thinking.

Maybe things didn't have to end after her grandmother's party.

Rafe held a plant in his hand as he leaned against the hood of his Porsche. He'd been waiting outside in the employees' parking lot at the Beach and Tennis Club for about ten minutes. Sarah should be finishing her shift at the restaurant any second now. It was only nine in the evening. They still had plenty of time left to dine on the supper he'd ordered set up on his balcony. Although he looked forward to the day she didn't work here at all.

With the plant and the dinner, he was trying to keep things low-key, the way Sarah said she preferred. Sex with Sarah had been mind-blowing—on the sofa, in his bed, again in the shower this morning.

And it hadn't been enough. He knew damn well a few days wouldn't be enough, either. He'd been with enough women to know that the connection with Sarah was something rare and he didn't intend to give it up. He wasn't going to give *her* up. They had great sex, similar backgrounds. He never had to worry she was after his money. He just needed to convince her.

If he played this her way for now, he would win in the long run. He needed to show her how she could have money and her simplicity. Then he could push for the more important issues like getting her to quit this job and move out of that damn house Quentin Dobbs had bought her.

Beyond keeping her safer, he wanted a commitment

from her. And hell yes, he wanted to separate her from the memories of the man she'd chosen over him.

His fist tightened around the plant so hard he had to force himself to chill before he cracked the terra-cotta pot. The past didn't matter. He had Sarah in his bed now, and no way in hell was he letting her go.

He heard her laugh on the wind before he saw her. His body went hard at just the sound of her voice. Luckily, the employees' lot was pretty deserted so he didn't have to ignore too many curious stares. Not that he'd ever cared much what people thought or said about him.

Then Sarah stepped in sight, waving goodbye to another waitress. He stopped thinking about anything else. She looked across to him and her smile widened.

God, he'd always liked her smile.

She didn't run or skip across the lot like she used to, but her walk was confident, her steps beating a steady tattoo along the asphalt. "I thought about you today."

Her husky voice wrapped around him a second before her arms looped around his neck.

"Good. I hope they were sex-filled thoughts that made you blush. And if not, then I look forward to the challenge of making that happen tonight." He kissed her hello with a quick brush across her lips that lingered a second longer than casual. He passed her the terra-cotta pot. "For you."

Her fingers glided across his neck, leaving a phantom sensation behind. "Oh, Rafe, it's a—"

"A Cereus plant." He'd sent his assistant to buy a tropical flower for Sarah's garden. Sure, he hadn't bought it himself, but he'd thought of the gift. "It blooms briefly, but magnificently. Like what we had back in high school."

She clutched it to her chest as if it was a freaking diamond necklace rather than a pot of dirt. "That's beautiful."

"I read it on a Hallmark card."

She batted at his shoulder. "No, you didn't."

"Maybe not." He slid past her to open the passenger-side door. "But I want to stay in your good graces, so I worked extra hard."

"You crave a challenge." Sarah slid into his car as she'd done hundreds of times in the past.

"I crave you." And he meant it. Soon, he would show her just how much.

Rafe settled behind the wheel and started the powerful 5.7-liter, V10 engine. What kind of car would Sarah pick when she chilled out enough to let him really start buying her things? Maybe he could cut a deal with her. For everything she let him buy her, he would donate that much to charity too. She would like that. She was seriously into the work Hannah's Hope was doing—

He stopped those thoughts in their tracks. He didn't want to think of his mother. Not now.

Sarah rested her plant on her knees. "Why the sudden change? All the romanticism and dates and drive to have me in your bed—not that I'm complaining about the sex part, mind you. But you managed to keep yourself well under control for the past five months around me."

"Stung your feelings, did it?" He turned the car onto the two-lane beach road, high on a bluff.

"You cannot be saying you ignored me on purpose. Even you can't be that Machiavellian. Can you?"

"I'm just here to give you a plant and a Hallmark moment. Although, I would give you more if you let me."

"Have you forgotten last night's argument about over-the-top gifts already?"

He eye stroked her for as long as he dared keep his eyes off the road. "What I want to give you isn't for sale."

Her chest rose and fell faster. She reached across the car and caressed his thigh, higher until she cupped—

He clasped her hand and brought her wrist up to his mouth. "Careful. I don't want to risk an accident or any more tickets from Officer Garcia. We'll be at my place in five minutes. Then you can do whatever you want with me."

"Do you really mean what you said?" Sarah asked softly. "Do you truly believe that the most meaningful things in life can't carry a price tag? That what we have is priceless?"

"Of course."

"Like what?"

"You want me to prove I'm not a materialistic jack-ass?" he glanced at her, cocking one eyebrow. "You want me to take a test?"

"I'm sorry. I didn't mean to hurt your feelings."

"You're admitting I have feelings." He laughed wryly. "That's progress."

She cradled the plant in her lap closer to her stomach.

"You have to admit, you've gone to a lot of trouble to cultivate that ruthless-corporate-raider image."

"Weakness rarely goes well at the bargaining table."

"Do you see keeping the plant open as a sign of weakness?"

She studied him so intently, so seriously, he had one of those déjà vu moments of his mom quizzing him in the second grade about how his shirt had gotten torn. He'd told her how he'd beaten the crap out of Quentin Dobbs for shoving Sarah off the monkey bars. Rafe had sworn he wasn't the least bit sorry because a real man defended the underdog.

He'd seen in his mother's eyes that she agreed, but she'd still made him apologize to Dobbs.

Unease prickled up his spine. But damn it, closing the plant made financial sense. Keeping it open only delayed the inevitable for those workers...the underdogs...

Crap.

He didn't want to think about this now. He wanted to focus on Sarah and keeping her by his side.

And in his bed.

Seven minutes later in the private elevator going up to his condo, he decided there was no time like the present. He backed her against the mirrored wall, angling his mouth over hers while he plucked the pins from her hair. A gust of her floral scent, her shampoo, filled him.

Without hesitation, she opened for him, cupping his ass and pulling him more fully against her. Her other hand stayed off to the side holding her plant, but the wriggle of her hips against his offered more than enough temptation to jack his heart rate right up.

The feel of her hair gliding over his fingers was the softest damn thing he'd ever known. Nothing matched Sarah.

Nothing.

And all that partnered with the drive-him-crazy visual of her melting all over him in the mirror just inches from his nose threatened to push him over the edge. His fingers made fast work of the buttons down her white shirt as the elevator doors whooshed open.

Without so much as breaking the kiss for a second, he walked her into the condo, their feet in perfect synch even in the building frenzy. He lifted the plant from her hand and placed it on the foyer table.

Four steps later they were in the dining room and he decided he couldn't wait a second longer. He tossed aside her shirt and unhooked her bra, flinging both aside. Her nipples were already tight and ready and inviting him to taste.

Her fingers tangled in his hair as she guided him toward her. "We're never going to make it to the bedroom at this rate."

"Not sure I care about that right now." Lifting her onto the mahogany dining table, he rubbed his beard-stubbled cheek against the side of her breast gently, reveling in her sigh of pleasure. "You're even more beautiful than before."

He braced his hands on the cool varnished table. Who'd have thought the lemony scent of furniture polish could be such a turn-on?

"Sarah, I thought of you so damn often." He nipped his way along her collarbone. "Usually late at night when I'm alone in some hotel, wishing like hell you could be there beside me, underneath me, on top of me."

He finished with a nip to her ear and dreamed of the day she would let him place big fat diamonds in place of the simple silver studs.

Her head fell back, exposing the graceful curve of her neck. "Honestly, you can't convince me you've been carrying around a torch for me for all these years." Her voice went breathy, with gaspy little hitches between her words. "The gossip columns are full of your dating exploits, from Hollywood starlets to wealthy debutantes."

Pausing, he tipped his head to meet her gaze. "You followed me in the papers?"

"That's not the point." Something shifted in her eyes. Jealousy? Uncertainty?

She couldn't possibly be freaking out over encounters they'd each had over the years. She wasn't the same inexperienced teen, either.

Still, something urged him to reassure her. "Half of it's made up. You remember how hard I work. I wouldn't have time for all the gossip reporters tagged me with doing." His forehead rested against hers. "But yes, I've seen other women, been with other women, but that doesn't keep you from slipping into my dreams."

The last admission was torn out of somewhere deep in his gut, a place he wasn't sure he wanted to admit to, even to himself. But she was doing something crazy to him, burning a path inside him that no other woman ever had.

"Oh Rafe," she said sadly, "I'm the one who got away. It's your competitive spirit speaking. This place, your car, it all says how much you want Vista del Mar to know you've won. Once we explore our unfinished business this week, you'll move on."

Unease gripped him by the throat. She was already talking about the end? Time with her was ticking away too fast and he didn't intend to waste a second convincing her. They were good together, damn it. And he knew just how to convince her he hadn't forgotten her, not for one second.

He slid her farther back on the table, sweeping aside the thick candlesticks and brass platter with a harsh clatter.

"Then come away with me." He stretched out over her, grateful as hell for the best sturdy flat surface money could buy. "Let's go somewhere neutral. I know just the place where we can explore all our unfinished business without any interruptions."

A knock on her front door interrupted Sarah as she planted the Cereus in her backyard.

She looked up quickly, hating how nervous she felt in her own home now. She'd made such a point of putting her foot down with Rafe about how she would be fine packing for their trip in broad daylight and now here she was, jumping like a scared rabbit.

She glanced at her suitcase under the patio table, then around the corner of the house to the front yard— and breathed a sigh of relief, recognizing Margaret Tanner's car.

"I'm out back, Margaret," Sarah called, peeling off her gardening gloves.

Margaret rounded the corner and jerked a thumb over her shoulder. "Why do you have a new front door? What happened to your other one?"

"Hello to you too, my friend." She swiped her wrist over her sweaty forehead then gestured to a seat at the patio table. "There was a break-in while I was out with Rafe, but they've already caught the guys who did it."

"Thank God you weren't home." She squeezed her friend's hand as they settled in across from each other. "And speaking of your date, that's why I'm here. How did it go?"

How much was she comfortable sharing? This all felt so new and strange, which was funny considering she'd known Rafe since they were kids. Might as well be up front. In a town this small, Margaret would likely find out anyway. Not to mention Margaret and her husband both worked for Rafe.

She reached under the wrought iron table to pull out her old battered suitcase, trying not to think of how she'd once packed it for her honeymoon. Two nights in a beach cottage in San Diego, a gift from her husband's parents. After Quentin had died, they'd both moved away to Northern California, unable to stay in Vista del Mar after losing their only child. They'd said they were unable to face the memories.

Sarah understood that also meant they were unable to face running into her.

Margaret's eyes went wide. "You're going on a trip?

You never go away on vacation, ever, not as long as I've known you."

"I'm taking time off from work." She could still hardly believe she'd said yes to his request that they go out of town. But then her brain hadn't been one hundred percent in gear when Rafe made love to her on the dining room table.

"About time you took a break." Margaret nodded approvingly, easing out of her sleek suit jacket in deference to the June heat. "Even when Quentin was alive, you only took day trips."

Her dead husband's name splashed cold water all over her memory from last night. "Money was tight."

"Money wasn't that tight." Margaret tapped the suitcase with the tip of her red Prada pumps. "So what's up now? That date must have gone really, really well."

For the first time in her life, Sarah found herself wondering if maybe designer shoes were more comfy than her bargain-basement flip-flops. "I'm just going away for a couple of days. I'll be back in time for Grandma Kat's birthday bash."

"You're going away with Rafe? Oh my God." She stretched across the table to squeeze both hands, her squeal almost as loud as the cars driving by out front. "This is too awesome."

"Maybe I'm taking my grandmother to a spa."

Margaret snorted on a laugh. "You know I'm going to have to call her right now."

"Don't. Please." She scrunched her toes in her sandals until they popped, trying not to notice her chipped pink polish. "I don't want to make a big deal out of this.... I'm not even a hundred percent sure why I said yes."

"Is he that amazing in bed?"

"I'm not answering that."

Margaret leaned back with a grin. "Too late. Your blush already answered for you."

God, she hated that telltale blush of hers. At thirty-two years old, she should be well past it. Most of all she worried though that Margaret could be right, that she was letting good sex—amazing sex—cloud her judgment.

The smile faded from Margaret's face, replaced by concern crinkling her brow. "You're really stressed over this."

"I'm not sure I'm making the right decision." It was one thing to decide on a few days of tantric sex. It was another altogether to leave town with him.

"You never overthink things. The fact that you're doing it now should tell you something."

"Like what."

"That this is important," Margaret said logically, as always one of the smartest people Sarah had ever met. "The higher the stakes, the bigger the risk."

"I don't love him anymore," she insisted. And hoped if she said it enough she could convince herself as well. "We're going to have a wild affair and put the past to rest. Or maybe it'll all fizzle out before the week's over and then I can let go of our high school romance."

Let go of Rafe. The thought stung like one of those bees buzzing around a hibiscus a few feet away.

"You know I'm totally gone on William, right? So

I don't mean anything inappropriate." Margaret and William Tanner's steamy affair and speedy wedding the past couple of months had rocked the gossip circles. "As a totally objective observer, I can still say without hesitation that there is nothing about Rafe Cameron that even hints of *fizzle out*."

Her eyes tracked to the Cereus plant Rafe had given her. Was their romance truly like that flower's brief bloom, or could Margaret be right that there might be something more?

She didn't have the answer to that now any more than she had fourteen years ago. She just prayed that there were some answers waiting for her in this mystery getaway Rafe had planned.

Nine

Rafe rinsed the shampoo from Sarah's hair, sweeping his hands down her back in long swipes. The shower in his private jet wasn't large, but it was big enough for the two of them. He'd made the most of their time airborne.

However, time was running out.

Reaching behind her, he turned off the shower. "We need to get dressed before we land."

She trailed her fingers down his chest. "It's your plane. Surely you can tell the pilot to circle the block a couple of extra times."

Chuckling, he clasped her wrist an inch shy of her distracting him for more than just a couple of extra loops around the runway. "Come on, you won't be sorry. There's an even better shower waiting where we're going."

He stepped out onto the Italian marble floor and snagged a monogrammed towel off a hook for her, then one for himself. As much as he wanted to take his time and dry her body off inch by gorgeous inch, he also wanted to show her the surprise waiting less than a mile from the runway.

Keeping his eyes well off her for now, he tugged on a pair of khakis and pulled a shirt over his head as he walked back into the main cabin. His jet sported all the equipment on board for a working office. For once, he'd delegated all his appointments to others in Cameron Enterprises. Chase had been stunned slack-jawed. William Tanner had smirked knowingly, but Rafe hadn't bothered with analyzing why—not with a plane to catch, a flight with Sarah.

She tugged her wet hair free of her long hippie dress. She'd always been a free spirit, one of the things he enjoyed about her back then. Now too, tugging on her wooden bead bracelets and sandals.

"Okay, Rafe, enough with the mystery." She gathered her hair and wrapped a long leather band around the long wet mass. "Where are we?"

"Nevada." He couldn't pull his eyes from her hands tying off the leather strip at the end. Who'd have thought watching her get dressed could be as sexy as watching her peel away her clothes? The intimacy of it twined around him, bringing a moment from the past of Sarah tugging up the straps of her bathing suit after a long-ago trip to the beach. The El Camino memories weren't all bad.

"Nevada?" She flipped the bound rope of hair over her shoulder and looked out the window. "Sure doesn't look much like Vegas out there." She pointed to the woodsy landscape, dark and deserted other than the lights along the single-lane runway.

His fingers itched to grasp her hips and pull her back against him. But the sooner he got her to his place, the sooner he would see her reaction. So he simply tucked his hands around her waist and eased her into her seat to belt in.

A smooth landing and shift over to the waiting car, he drove her to his vacation home, only a couple of minutes from the private airstrip. If they'd arrived during the day, she would have seen the place from the sky. But he'd planned it this way. He wanted her to be surprised. He'd never expected to have this moment with her and he wanted to savor every second of her reaction.

He stopped the Mercedes SUV in front of the un-obtrusive—but highly secure—gate. He lowered the electric window and punched in the code that disarmed the alarm and turned on...

The lights.

Sarah gasped beside him, sitting up straighter in her seat. She gripped the dash and stared out through the windshield. "A woodsy, homey cabin that has high ceilings with big fat beams," she said, repeating the words she'd said to him fourteen years ago when describing her dream vacation home.

"And windows that take up an entire wall." He finished her sentence as she gawked at the log cabin built into a mountainside.

For an instant worry stabbed through him that she might be upset at him for building *her* dream house without her, that she might wonder about other women tromping through. But this was his private retreat. No one except him and basic caretakers had come through.

He hadn't even finished the place yet because he hadn't known how to. She hadn't described much more than the outside. He started to explain—

She turned to him, awe and tears in her eyes. "You built it exactly like we dreamed about. You actually remembered that one conversation we had fourteen years ago?"

"I remember everything you said." And he was working his ass off here to let her know he was determined to keep her around this time. Things would be easier now that he could bankroll her dreams. "About how you didn't want to stay in impersonal hotels. You loved home and hominess. We decided a vacation house would suit you better."

She slumped back in her seat, her hand pressed to her heart. "I'm blown away, you know."

"Good. That was completely my intention." He unlocked the car doors. "Now come inside with me so you can see the rest."

Her heart in her throat, Sarah stepped into the wide-open gathering space of the log cabin, her dream vacation home. She trailed her fingers along the rough-hewn wood. The bottom floor was an open-concept living area, dining space and kitchen with rustic walls and the largest stone fireplace she'd ever seen. The ceiling soared up to a second story. Through the railing she could see a long hall of doors, at least four bedrooms.

But the place was empty other than a table with a computer and a fat recliner angled beside the fireplace to look out the massive wall of windows.

She spun to face him. "If you wanted a vacation home, why haven't you decorated it?"

"What would you suggest?" He leaned a shoulder against the mantel that looked like a reclaimed barn beam.

"Two overstuffed leather sofas and huge wood rocking chairs. Plenty of seating, for sure. And quilts draped everywhere. Maybe one on the wall, as well." Her mind filled with possibilities and she hadn't even finished with the first room. "But you don't need my feedback. You can afford the best interior decorator."

"What if I *want* you to outfit the space?"

Her stomach flipped with nerves. "I doubt we can furnish this place in a couple of days."

"Then we'll take longer," he said, deceptively still. "You should choose the rest of the details. The house you designed has been waiting for you."

She gripped the back of the recliner, her knees suddenly weak. "Don't play games with me here. You're moving way too fast. This was supposed to be about spending a little time together. We would discuss alternatives to closing the factory—"

He pressed a finger to her lips. "And we can talk. All you want. But why do we have to rush? The factory's important. What's happening between us is important. Why shouldn't we take more than a few days to address such important issues?" he asked with such cool logic it gave her pause.

She didn't want their time together to become some

calculated prospect, but he had a point about taking their time. And more time together would give her a chance to discuss the factory.

It would give her more time in his arms, too. "I have to confess, I don't really want to have the corporate raider fight right now."

"I don't want to argue with you at all." He shoved away from the mantel and extended a hand. "Walk with me. There's more to see in the back."

Grateful for the diversion, she strolled alongside him. The last thing she wanted was to waste this time arguing. He guided her through the living area, steady footsteps echoing. Sliding doors opened to a massive balcony perched on a mountainside. A cool summer breeze carried the scent of pines. He flipped a switch and tiny white lights twinkled along the balcony.

A sound system piped in vintage tunes from their high school era. The disco ball with planets spinning around it confirmed her impression. Two porch loungers with poofy cushions bracketed a small refreshments table.

She clapped a hand over her mouth, twirling to take it all in, let the enormity of what he'd done sink in. This gesture really took her back a step, making her question if the old Rafe was more alive than she'd given him credit for.

The silky fabric of her dress caressed her calves as she stood still again. "You've recreated our senior prom?"

"That's the idea." He drew her to the middle of the balcony. "Dance with me, Sarah."

Stepping into his arms, she synched her steps with

his. Seeing this house, feeling his arms strong and familiar around her, she could almost resurrect hopes from the past. Maybe she hadn't imagined that he could blend his working-man roots with this high-powered mogul lifestyle he craved.

His hands roved her back, tucking her closer with each fluid move. "Do you realize how tough it was to hold back in those days?" He toyed with the end of her damp ponytail. "How much I wanted you?"

"I would have given you everything that night."

He nuzzled her temple. "You were drunk. That wouldn't have been fair."

Again, his innate honor made her optimistic that maybe he could let go of his vendetta against Ronald Worth. Maybe finally he could accept that he was a regular guy from a regular family. An amazing family. His father, Bob, and stepmother, Penny, were there for him. So was Chase.

Her mind drifted back to prom night, beyond when she'd thrown herself at Rafe, tipsy from the spiked punch. But to later, at his house….

In Rafe's kitchen, Sarah cradled the mug of coffee, her third, and sipped the kick-butt strong brew. She didn't feel a hundred percent steady yet, but at least the refrigerator had stopped wobbling from side to side. She hadn't wanted him to bring her to his father and his dad's fiancée, Penny, but Rafe had insisted it was here, or go home to face Grandma Kat.

So here she sat in her prom dress, with her corsage wilting as fast as her buzz. "I am so embarrassed."

Penny nudged aside the stack of textbooks on the

table and patted her hand. "It's not your fault someone spiked the punch."

Bob's fiancée was a nice lady, kinda quirky, but Sarah actually liked that about her. And Penny was clearly devoted to Bob. The woman rarely took her eyes off her Harrison-Ford-look-alike fiancé.

Did the adults believe she hadn't known the punch was spiked? She cringed that they might think she was lying. Their approval was really important to her. These two people would be her family forever once she and Rafe got married.

Would Bob and Penny stay in Vista del Mar? She knew that Bob had been looking for a better job since he got his GED. Her hands trembled around the mug as she thought of everything changing so fast. Would there be anything familiar to return to here?

The linoleum floor vibrated under her feet and it had nothing to do with any alcohol this time. Car headlights swept through the window, tires crunching as the vehicle pulled into the driveway.

Rafe frowned. "Who would be coming here at midnight?"

Penny looked down and away quickly. Bob clapped his son on the shoulder, an apology already stamped all over his face.

Penny covered Sarah's hand and patted. "Your grandmother is here, honey."

Rafe jerked away from his father, anger radiating off him in waves. Sarah shot to her feet, jostling the table. She grabbed the edge to keep from swaying. The stack of textbooks slid to the side, spreading tourism flyers about Los Angeles across the table.

Tears stung her eyes over how the whole evening had fallen apart, but she blinked them back. She busied herself with gathering up a couple of maps of L.A. while she blinked away the moisture. The last thing she needed was for Rafe to get more upset, and no doubt if he saw her crying, he would grow angrier. God, she wanted to drop-kick that little Jason or whoever was responsible for spiking the punch.

Bob opened the squeaky screen door just as her grandmother stepped inside. Grandma Kat had passed down her red hair—and her temper—to Sarah. From the look of her grandma's tightly pressed lips, the temper was simmering close to the surface.

"Sarah," her grandmother said tersely. "Time to go home."

"Rafe will take me." She stood her ground. Rafe might not be much like his family. But there was no mistaking Sarah was completely, through and through, a Richards.

Kathleen Richards's gaze zipped from her to her date then back to her again. "I think it's best that you come with me now."

"Someone spiked the punch at the prom," she said slowly, carefully. "He brought me straight here for coffee, like a responsible date."

Her grandmother brushed her feet on the doormat and walked farther into the room. "These people aren't your family or legal guardians, which is why they called me. Rafe should have brought you home. If you had nothing to hide, there wouldn't have been a problem, now would there?"

Her face burned with a flush of anger over her

grandmother's refusal to believe her. "I'm a senior in high school, only a month away from graduating and being on my own."

"Almost on your own. But not quite." She waved a hand toward the door. "Sarah, get in the car."

Rafe stood tall and tense, his jaw tight as he faced her grandmother, strongly but respectfully. "Ma'am, I am sorry. You trusted me with your granddaughter and I let you down."

"Thank you for the apology," Kathleen answered, some of the starch going out of her spine. And then her eyes narrowed. "Young man, one of the best things in life a person can learn is when you're in over your head. Tonight, you were in over your head with Sarah. Think about it. Now if you'll excuse me, Sarah should be at home, with her family."

Her grandmother wrapped an arm around her shoulders and steered her toward the door. Sarah looked back at Rafe, pleading with her eyes. Their prom night couldn't end this way. He should charge in, claim her, declare they were a couple. They were going to leave together after graduation.

But he didn't say a word. He didn't even walk with her to the car. As she sat in the front seat of her grandmother's old boat-size sedan, she watched in the rearview mirror as Rafe simply closed the door without so much as a glance of regret her way.

She scraped a sliding spaghetti strap back up and tried not to think about how she'd almost tossed away her clothes and her virginity tonight. She'd been ready to give him everything, her body, her heart, her future. She'd been so certain he cared about her as much as *she loved him when he didn't take advantage of her offer on Busted Bluff.*

But now she wondered if he'd stopped for another reason. Her mind skated back to those flyers and maps of Los Angeles mixed in with his textbooks. She'd assumed it must be for a school project, but now she wondered if he'd been making plans to go already, without even talking to her. He had to know a big city like that would be dead last on her list. She couldn't ignore the niggling sense that he was holding back in their relationship so he would have fewer regrets after graduation when he left town....

Without her....

Rafe felt Sarah stiffen in his arms as they danced under the moonlight. "Whatever you're thinking about, stop."

He wanted to relax her with the mountain-backdrop setting, the home he'd built just for her. The place had been intended as more of a catharsis originally, a way to work regrets out of his system. But having her here, he knew the home had been waiting for her.

Still, something had shifted inside her, taken away the joy pulsing from her when she'd first entered the house.

"Sarah?" he prodded.

"Just remembering our senior prom." She looked up at him, her half smile shaky.

The power of her allure that night steamrolled him again, along with other concerns they'd had in those days—concerns that would have made his life and plans even more complicated. "And I didn't want to risk getting you pregnant."

A delicate eyebrow arched as she shuffled her feet in time to the old Celine Dion tune. "Didn't you carry around a condom in those days?"

"I did after that." He twirled her past the two patio loungers then swept her into a dip.

She laughed lightly, the sound mingling with the trickle of a distant mountain stream.

He gathered up her thick mass of hair, looping it around his wrist and holding her closer. "Why don't you have any children?"

"Why don't you have any manners?" Her smile faded.

Damn. He hadn't meant to kill the mood that way but the question had just fallen from his mouth. Maybe he had some subliminal need to know there was a darker reason than just waiting for the right time. He didn't want her to have loved Dobbs the way she'd once said she loved him.

He was a jerk for even thinking it. "If you don't want to answer, just say so."

Her feet slowed, then stopped. She pulled out of his arms and walked to the balcony rail, keeping her back to him. "Quentin and I tried. It was difficult to conceive and even when I did, I miscarried early on."

God, he was an even bigger selfish jackass than he'd thought. He hadn't even considered this when he'd thoughtlessly waded into the conversation. Her stony profile and rigid spine shouted loud and clear how much he'd upset her by forcing this conversation.

He stood beside her at the balcony overlooking the

rocky drop-off. "I am so sorry. Sorry for bringing it up and sorry for the pain you went through. You should have your arms full of redheaded children with your amazing smile."

"Yes, I should." Her lips went tight with tension before she blurted, "I should also still have my husband alive, but I can't change any of that. Do I have regrets? Absolutely. I've had three years to live with those feelings. I've come to the conclusion a part of my heart will always feel that pain, but I have to keep going."

Sniffling, she scraped her wrist over her eyes brusquely, still refusing to look at him.

He leaned on his elbows, staring out at the view he'd chosen a year ago with her in mind, even if he hadn't realized it at the time. "I came to see you once."

"When?" She looked at him sharply, finally. "How did I not know?"

"Two years after I left." The day kicked back over him now, how much he'd missed her, more than he'd thought possible. He'd caved. "The opportunity had come up to move to New York and I knew that you weren't going to want to live there any more than you wanted to live in Los Angeles, but I figured what the hell? I would give it a try and ask."

"Two years... I would have been engaged to or just married to Quentin."

"Still engaged, just before you married him." He'd heard about the engagement and it was driving him nuts. "I had this crazy ass idea about talking to you before you tied the knot. I would persuade you to reconsider. It was around the Fourth of July and you were at some festival. It was all small-town and hokey and you were loving every minute of it."

He had her complete attention now, for certain. She stared up at him, moonlight glinting off her wide, confused jade eyes.

Rafe tapped the corner of her mouth. "You even had a little red bit of cotton candy right there. And it struck me. Quentin Dobbs had the right to kiss that away. Not me. Not anymore. You'd made your choice, one that would give you everything you ever wanted."

"I wanted you," she whispered, turning her face into his hand. "I was willing to go with you and Bob and Penny to L.A."

"So you say, but you balked at the last minute, insisting it wasn't what I really wanted. Would you have walked away if I'd agreed to come back to this tiny town and doom us both to poverty for the rest of our lives?"

She nodded sadly. "Rafe, I know your mother's death was difficult for you, but plenty of people make it big in places other than New York and L.A." She clutched his shirt. "I think you're using that as an excuse. If you'd really loved me, you would have given us time to figure out a compromise. You didn't have to leave for L.A. right away just because Bob and Penny were going."

Anger snapped inside him. He was flaying himself raw for her here, telling her things he'd never told anyone, showing Sarah this house. "You can accuse me of a lot of things, being a jerk, being selfish—" he closed his hands over hers, carefully pulling her grip free "—but don't ever deny that I loved you then, damn it."

As he turned away before his temper got the best of him, she grabbed his shoulder. "I'm sorry."

He glanced back at her. "For what, exactly?"

"For all the ways we hurt each other."

Tears swam in her eyes even as her shoulders stayed braced and strong. All the roiling feelings from back then merged with the present. The intense need to be with her, inside her, roared through him.

Sarah stepped toward him, just one step but that's all it took. His mouth was on hers, claiming her now as he hadn't all those years ago. She tore at his shirt. The buttons gave way, popped and rained down on the floor. Night air brushed his chest a second before her lips were on him, kissing, tasting, nipping with an urgency echoed in him.

Bunching her dress in his fists, he inched the fabric up, up farther still until he pulled the silky mass over her head. She gasped and he covered her lips with his finger.

"No worries. We're completely private here." He dropped the dress to the deck and took in the beauty of Sarah in nothing but yellow silk panties and a matching strapless bra. "Do you think I would let anyone else see you?"

With a deft slide of his hand behind her back, he slid her bra away and pulled her to him. Music and memories wrapped around him as he danced her over to the lounger. Her breasts grazed his chest with each step until he wasn't sure if the moans of pleasure came from his throat or hers. Either way, his body was on fire for her.

Kicking aside their shoes, her panties, his slacks, he lowered her to the wide patio lounger. A big bed waited upstairs, but so many times in the past they'd almost made love under the stars. Finally they would live out that fantasy in their fantasy home.

She opened her arms for him, her body already arching toward him with urgency. He reached for his wallet and pulled out a condom. Grief flickered through her eyes and he kissed each lid closed. He would take away all her heartache if he could.

But right now, all he could give her was himself. He slid inside her. The feel of her around him threatened to finish him too soon, but he held back, determined to draw out this fantasy-come-true for as long as possible.

He'd spent most of his teenage years fantasizing about all the ways he wanted to make love to Sarah, but outside under an open sky had always been one of his favorites. The stars glittered over her bare skin like tiny diamonds. And as much as he wanted to look at her all damn night, he wanted to taste her even more.

Taking one pert nipple in his mouth, he savored the way she reacted to the flick of his tongue, going pebbly hard in a flash. She writhed against him. Their bodies synched up in perfect rhythm.

In a fluid move, he rolled onto his back, settling her on top of him without ever once losing the mind-blowing connection of his body in hers. Her hot moist core clamped around him, drew him in her deeper.

And how perfect that now he could look his fill while stroking her to the fullest.

He cradled her creamy breasts in his hands, eliciting a moan from her damp lips. She stroked over him with frantic, soft hands, her touch growing more urgent, her fingernails rasping along his arms. Her chest rose and fell faster, flushing with pleasure as she rode him harder, faster, taking him as completely as he took her. Her head fell back as she rolled her hips and just the sight of the two of them joined threatened to send him over the edge.

Sarah, Sarah, Sarah. Her name pulsed through his veins, resonated in his ears so loudly he realized he'd chanted her name aloud. She was perfect. The only woman who'd ever moved him this way.

The only woman who ever would.

Something snapped inside him and he couldn't hold back. But no way was he going over the edge without her. His hand slid down between them, between her thighs, slicking the dampness of her desire over the tight bundle of nerves, circling, plucking, working her until…

Her beautiful cries of completion washed over him and finally, finally he could follow her right over the edge, free-falling into the explosion consuming him, her, both of them together, until she melted over him.

Her body blanketed him as he panted in the aftermath. Sweat slicked their bodies, sealing them together, stirring an erotic scent in the fresh night air. The rightness of being here, being with her, settled over him.

Sarah. It was all about Sarah and always had been. He'd been deluding himself to think otherwise.

Buried deep inside her, damn near drunk on the softness of her all around him, he cradled her face in his hands. "Marry me."

Ten

Rafe's question was like a splash of cold water.

Sarah's body chilled from the inside out. "What did you say?"

He stroked back her hair, his intensely blue eyes lit by the stars and disco ball. "Marry me."

The tingling passion faded as he brought reality into their fantasy. She didn't know what prompted him to say that, but a marriage proposal tied up with sex didn't ring true.

She rolled her hips against his. "In case you didn't notice, we've already had sex, more than once. I'm trying to go for it again right now." And it obviously wasn't working. She slid from beneath him. "You don't have to propose to get me into bed."

Or onto the patio lounger.

"That's not why I asked you to marry me the night we

graduated, right before I left town." He sat, unabashedly nude and turned on. "And your reaction now is far from flattering."

He was right. She couldn't blame him so much when he was bending and she found she wasn't ready. She had to take ownership of her own walls she was putting up between them because of her reservations—her fears. Still, he must know...

"Proposals that come out in the heat of the moment are not all that reliable. This is something I can't take lightly." She grabbed her clothes and tossed his pants into his lap.

"Neither do I." He watched her through narrowed eyes as she tugged on her underwear. "I didn't propose back then just to get you into bed."

"Of course you did." She yanked her dress on then dropped to the edge of a lounger. "I essentially issued an ultimatum, wedding ring for sex. We were tied up in knots from waiting so long."

"We'd become fairly adept at taking the edge off." He tugged his khakis up and sat beside her.

The heat of his leg against hers, his broad bare chest a simple reach away tempted her as much as the memories of how they'd pleasured each other. She wished they were entertaining some of those options now instead of having this unsettling conversation. This was supposed to be about sex and getting him to change his mind about closing the factory, not launching headfirst into marriage. Why was he even doing this? It wasn't like he'd declared undying love for her.

She leaned into his chest, praying she could just

distract him. "Let's go inside and see the rest of the house."

He linked his fingers with hers but he didn't stand. "I understood it was important to you back then to wait until you were married."

All of a sudden she knew exactly where he was taking this conversation. She did not want to venture down that path. Not with Rafe and certainly not with the scent of him still clinging to her.

Rafe's hand twitched holding hers, giving her only a second's warning.

"Was Quentin your first?"

Her scalp tingled, pulling tight until her brain felt vise-gripped. She snatched her hand away. "You don't have any right to ask that."

"I'm not known for my tact."

She stood abruptly, searching for an escape in the middle of nowhere.

Standing, he clasped her fingers again to stop her. "Let's quit talking. We'll lie here together and look at the stars."

She yanked her hand away, spinning to face him. She could see her reflection in his eyes and barely recognized herself with her frantic expression and tousled hair. She was known for her temper, but never had she felt this out of control, this raw.

"Yes, I had my wedding night with Quentin, my first, and he was a caring, tender lover. And afterward," her breath hitched at the visions in her head, "I slipped away into the bathroom to hide and cry my eyes out. Because even though he made my body respond, and he was everything a bride could have wanted on her wedding night, he wasn't you."

She watched Rafe's fists go white-knuckled. Otherwise he stayed completely still and quiet. But his eyes, his beautiful blue eyes were awash with jealousy and guilt and something else she couldn't define.

Or maybe she wasn't ready to face it yet.

Her knees were quivering as much as her insides, but there was no stopping now. "Everyone thinks I'm so emotional, and most of the time, like now, that's true. But I also understand the importance of making a decision, of committing to that decision and sticking with it."

She gasped in steadying breaths of the beautiful mountain air she'd only dreamed about before, and as much as she was moved by what he'd done for her with his millions, it still didn't erase the past. How could she trust him not to push her aside again if he felt his "kingdom" was threatened? He didn't understand love and commitment the same way she did.

"I loved Quentin and I chose to make our life together work and have meaning. You say you loved me, but you chose your ambition when you forced us to make a decision on graduation night. We were eighteen years old, for God's sake. What was so wrong with taking a summer to plan out our life?"

"I proposed to you, damn it."

She shook her head slowly. "I told you then and I still believe it now, you didn't really want to marry me. That was only our hormones speaking. Don't try to rewrite history now and pretend otherwise."

His head snapped back at her last words as if she'd

slapped him. And maybe she reveled in that just a little, finally making the almighty Rafe Cameron hear he couldn't buy everything.

Yet more than anything, she wanted him to reassure her that he'd changed. He'd learned from the past and truly wanted to make that future with her. Yes, she wanted to marry him, but for the right reasons.

She waited for him to answer, could almost see him lining up his response in his mind. A calculated reply? Or an answer from the heart?

A ringing sounded, startling her.

Rafe tipped his head, and she realized his cell phone was ringing from the refreshment table.

"Take that call," she said, weary and frustrated.

"We're talking, damn it."

The anger icing his words didn't make her all that inclined to continue chitchatting. She grabbed the phone and thrust it toward him. "Answer the phone. It's probably work." She glanced at the name on the faceplate. *Chase Larson.* "It's…your stepbrother."

Frowning, Rafe took the phone from her and answered with a clipped, "Better be an emergency, bro, because I am beyond busy."

His frown deepened and he plowed his hand through his hair. "Right, of course, I'm so damn sorry. You go be with Emma. I've got everything covered. I'm on my way back as we speak."

He thumbed the phone off, his face a serious scowl that sent a bolt of foreboding through her stomach. Emma Larson was pregnant, about seven months along. Sarah fought for air as she thought of her own miscarriages, how easily a precious young life could flicker out.

Rafe pocketed his phone. "We need to leave. Emma just went to the hospital. The doctor thinks it's premature labor."

Rafe stared out the window in his office at Cameron Enterprises—formerly Worth Industries. Vista del Mar was now his to do with as he wished and yet none of that meant a damn when he thought of his stepbrother up at that hospital fearing for his wife and child.

Plowing his hand through his hair, he couldn't help but think of how he would feel if that was Sarah in the hospital. She'd told him of her multiple miscarriages. God, what if something had happened to her?

What if she suffered like that again in the future?

There was no bully on the playground for him to beat up on her behalf. There were honest-to-God things he couldn't fix for Sarah.

Things he couldn't fix for Chase and Emma.

After Chase's phone call, Rafe and Sarah had packed quickly, no time for talking. His plane had them home before sunrise. Sarah had obviously been rattled by the call just as he had. And he couldn't miss how talk of Dobbs had obviously upset her, so much so that Rafe couldn't ignore how much her dead husband had meant to her. She hadn't just married him on the rebound. She'd genuinely loved the guy and had wanted to build a life and a family with him.

His jealous need to be number one in her mind had made him push her when she obviously wasn't ready. He didn't have a right to know those things about her marriage, not now. He hadn't earned his way back into her life yet, and he was a fool to think a few days erased years apart.

God, his strategy was all over the map. When the hell had he lost his ability to focus on the objective?

He'd waited over half his life to stand in this office. From the day he'd realized his mother was ill and working in that plant had likely caused it. She'd put off going to the doctor because money was tight. Then she'd left it too late.

There was nothing doctors could do for Hannah except make her as comfortable as possible while the COPD ravaged her body. She'd only been thirty-five years old and died of lung failure from working in that damn factory as a teenager.

Finally, he was in a position to crush that factory to dust. And right now, all he could think about was how much he wanted to be with Sarah, together, supporting his stepbrother up at the hospital.

The phone buzzed and his secretary announced, "Ronald Worth is here to see you, Mr. Cameron."

Ronald Worth? What the hell? Surprise jolted Rafe all the way to his loafers...then it hit him. Worth was Emma's father. Had he come here to deliver news Chase was too devastated to pass along?

Damn.

"Send him in." He turned away from the door to gather his composure before he faced his lifelong adversary.

The door clicked open and he heard footsteps, heavy, slower than he would have expected, but Worth was getting older, in his midsixties now. All that blond hair he'd passed on to his children was stark-silver now.

Worth stepped alongside him, hands behind his back as the two men stood shoulder to shoulder. They were even the same height. Worth's chair had been set just right for Rafe when he'd taken the helm of the company, as if easing the way for him to have his vengeance.

The older businessman had been every bit as ruthless in his day. Rafe reminded himself this man was here as a father now, not a ruthless businessman. "How's Emma?"

"She's fine, the baby too. Apparently it was something called Braxton Hicks, not real labor. The doctors are having her take it easy just to be safe given the problems she had early on in the pregnancy."

"Thank God." Rafe exhaled in relief. Then surprise knocked around in the aftermath. "Why are you here then? Why not call?"

Worth rocked back on his heels. "I wanted to take this chance to speak to you alone. A conversation between us is long overdue."

Alarms jangled in his head. He should have known not to lower his guard, even for a second, around this bastard. Who the hell knew what Worth would pull out of his arsenal?

Ronald cleared his throat. "All pride is out the window for me now. You've won and we both know it."

Rafe waited for the rush of victory, but the world just seemed…quiet. "Then why are you here?"

"I am pleading with you not to close the factory."

"That's it? That's your big pitch?" Either the old guy

was losing it or he'd been one lucky bastard to make it so far. "I'm a businessman. This is a business decision."

"If I thought that was the case, I wouldn't bother speaking with you." Worth turned toward him, his chin high in spite of his humbled position. "Your resentment of me, of my company, has never been a secret."

"And your point is?" Rafe met him eye to eye.

"A good businessperson makes decisions with all the facts in front of him." He hesitated, looking around the office that used to be his. "You are missing critical information."

Damn. He should have known the old goat still had something up his sleeve. "My lawyer isn't going to like this." He reached for his cell phone. "He should be present for this discussion."

"Hold off." Worth raised a hand, spotted with age but still steady. "This has nothing to do with attorneys. There's no easy way to say this but the scare with Emma today made me realize that I can't delay any longer. Life is too fragile. I need to tell you something…."

"Then get to it. I don't have all day." Rafe couldn't help but wonder why he wasn't reveling more in this groveling he'd been waiting for.

Maybe there was something to what Sarah had said about his vendetta being out of control. He'd let this man hijack his life long enough. "If you don't have anything substantial to offer up, I'm going to have to ask you to leave."

Rafe started toward the door.

Worth gripped his arm. "The real reason your mother left Worth Industries—the reason she was let go—was because she and I had an affair."

Worth's hand fell away, but Rafe was too shocked to notice. So much so he barely processed that Worth was still speaking.

"I was married and my wife found out. She became… unhinged with jealousy." Worth stuffed his hands into his pockets and began pacing, his shoulders slumping. "She was going to take away my children—I was going to lose Emma and Brandon. The only way I could save my marriage, the only way to keep my family together, was if I agreed to cut your mother out of my life."

It had to be a ploy. That was the only explanation. No way in hell would his mother have hooked up with this cold, heartless ass. "My mother was already with my father then. You fired them for fraternizing. Her pregnancy was your 'proof.'"

Worth stared at him without speaking, blue eyes intense.

Her pregnancy.

A lightning strike split through Rafe's skull. Worth had lobbed a bomb into his being without even articulating the allegation.

His mother's pregnancy. A pregnancy that happened at the same time as this alleged affair. "No way. No damn way will I believe I am your kid." To hell with the fact they both had blond hair and blue eyes while no one in his family was fair-headed. Worth was just using that genetic throwback to his advantage. "You're only trying this to keep me from shutting Worth Industries, and I have to say it's mighty damn low, even for you."

"I should have told you a long time ago." Worth sagged onto the sofa, age lines creasing his face. "Especially once my wife died. A part of me kept

hoping Hannah or Bob would tell you so I wouldn't
have to. Not very honorable of me, but then my behavior
has been far from exemplary from the start."

Rafe resisted the urge to pinch the bridge of his nose,
right along where his headache was building. But he
refused to show any vulnerability around this man. "Let
me get this straight. You, a married man, had an affair
with my mother, got her pregnant, then fired her as well
as the man you say stepped in to be a father to your
bastard child."

"That pretty much sums it up." He fidgeted with a
cuff link nervously. "If you still don't believe me, ask
Bob."

Bob. His father. Not his father? Bile churned in his
gut, burning up his throat. God, he felt sick. Because
it was beginning to sink in that this could be true.
Why would Worth send him to confirm it with Bob
otherwise? In this day of DNA tests, paternity couldn't
be faked.

"And if all of that's true, why in the hell would it
make me more sympathetic to you?" He grabbed the
old man by the shirtfront and hauled him closer. "If
anything, I want to crush you into the ground for what
you did to my mother."

Worth didn't even fight back. "I'm the one you want
revenge against, not the employees who worked for me,
not a whole factory full of people just like your mother
and Bob. You're my son, but don't be like me. Don't
make others suffer because of your own issues."

Rage pounded through him, beyond anything he'd
felt—and he'd hated Ronald Worth for a lot of years.
And now this disgusting man might be his father? Rafe

released the bastard's shirt abruptly and Worth crumpled down onto the sofa.

Worth's head fell into his hands. "For what it's worth, I loved your mother. I genuinely believed she and the baby—you—were better off with Bob." He plowed his hands through his silver hair then looked up at Rafe. "I did what I thought was best to protect all three of my children."

And then it hit him that Emma and Brandon could be—likely were—his half sister and half brother. He'd once called Emma "The Spawn of Satan" and now it appeared he carried that title as well.

God, this was all too much on top of how his relationship with Sarah was coming apart at the seams. He had to get away. Now. His feet carried him out the door and for the first time in his life, he didn't have a clue where to go.

Disarming her newly installed security system, Sarah opened her replaced front door, desperate to hear what had happened with Emma.

While her temper had cooled some in light of what was going on with Chase and Emma, Sarah still wasn't budging. They needed to take things slower. Delving into such deep emotional waters so soon was dangerous. They had a lot of time to make up for, a lot of ground to cover first. They still hadn't resolved the issue about how to save the factory...or some other way to find jobs for all those faithful employees who would be out of a job.

Her door swung wide and as always, just seeing him took her breath away. He filled the frame with his broad shoulders. While he ruled the boardroom, he still kept his body as honed as his mind.

And all of those muscles were tightly tensed, visibly bunched under his shirt. His jacket was nowhere to be seen and his tie was loosened. His scowl would stop a train.

"Oh my God…is Emma okay?"

He squeezed her shoulder. "She and the baby are both fine. False alarm, thank God."

Sagging with relief, Sarah stepped back for him to enter then closed the door. "That had to have been so scary for them all the same." She swallowed down a lump, keeping her eyes off her wedding photo. "Rafe? Is something else wrong?"

"I met with Worth today." Rafe charged restlessly around her tiny living room like a caged lion, feet thudding along her braid rug. "He made a last-ditch effort to convince me not to shutter the factory."

Wow, not what she'd expected to hear, but now that the subject was out there, perhaps the time had finally come to seriously address the need. "And this discussion with Mr. Worth obviously bothered you. It's tough once we allow those faces to become more personal." Maybe he was finally understanding the impact of his actions in closing the plant. Maybe finally his heart was opening after all.

"You're misunderstanding." His fingers tapped restlessly along her mantel, hesitating in front of a wedding photo. He turned away abruptly. "He didn't pull any punches. He said that the scare with Emma and her pregnancy made him realize he needed to come clean.

He told me… He told me that he and my mother had an affair."

Sarah gasped, her legs folding. She sat on the arm of her sofa by the basket of clean laundry. "What a despicable lie. Hannah never would have cheated on Bob."

"An affair before my fath— Before Bob." The room wasn't big enough to contain his growing agitation. "He said that the real reason he fired my mother was because his wife made it a condition of forgiving him for the affair."

Even though she couldn't accept it was true, she could see it clearly had rocked Rafe. She shoved to her feet and rested her hand on his arm to stop him, soothe him. "That had to be so shocking to hear. Why would he tell you something like that? What does he have to gain?"

And how had a secret like that managed to stay undiscovered in this small town? Surely her grandmother would have said something.

Her mind echoed with memories of standing in the Worth mansion foyer, of hearing her grandmother implore Ronald to tell Rafe the truth….

Foreboding burned through her. "What else did he say?"

"He told me that he is my biological father." The revelation hissed through his gritted teeth. "He said that Bob married my mother so I wouldn't be born a bastard."

"Rafe, I'm so sorry." She wrapped her arms around his waist, holding tight even though he stood stock-still.

"I can't even begin to imagine how hard that must have been to hear."

"That my archenemy is really my father? I feel like I'm stuck in some sick remake of *Star Wars,* for God's sake." His laugh was dark and hard, not anything like the tender lover of the past days. "The man I called 'Dad' all these years has been lying to me, along with my mother? Yeah, I would call that difficult."

She tried to guide him to the sofa to sit, but he was an immovable mountain. "Rafe, let's take a deep breath. It's too much to absorb at once. Have you talked to Bob? I really think you should speak to him."

Rafe stepped out of her arms as if she hadn't even spoken, cricking his neck from side to side. "Well, Worth made his big confession for nothing. It doesn't change a thing. If anything, it gives me all the more reason to hammer that godforsaken plant into the ground."

"Rafe! You can't mean that." She squeezed his arm for emphasis, for impact, to make some kind of connection that would get through to him.

"Like hell I don't." The venom in his voice chilled her clean through. "He used my mother then tossed her away. Even when she was dying, he still didn't lift a finger to help her. He's the bastard here and he deserves to pay for everything he's done."

She squeezed harder, desperate to get through to him, to hold on to the hope that had only just started to grow within her. "But other people don't deserve to suffer because of your hatred for him."

"The world isn't some little Utopia, Sarah." He looked down at her with cool cynicism. "Your Vista del Mar fantasy is just that. A fantasy. Some castle-in-the-sky dream, but it's time to come down to earth now, Kitten. This is the way the world works."

Every word out of his mouth affirmed her reservations about him and what he wanted from life. The past few days had been an…anomaly, at best. And at worst? A calculated effort on his part.

So much for the flights of fancy about working things out with him. About being part of his life for more than just a week. His heart had hardened so much she couldn't imagine him ever letting her inside.

"Oh Rafe," she said, sighing her regret, her heartbreak, "you haven't changed a bit."

"I haven't changed?" He cocked an eyebrow. "You live in the same town, working the same job, closing your eyes and mind to anything that doesn't fit the mold."

Her hands fell away from him, her head snapping back. "You're being deliberately cruel because you're hurting," she said carefully, her own temper starting to simmer. "I can understand and forgive in light of the circumstances, but you really need to put the brakes on your mouth."

"Back when we dated, you wanted me to talk more. Well, this is what I have to say. This is who I am." He flattened a hand to his chest. "Face up to it or turn away with your hands over your ears like you did fourteen years ago."

Was that how he saw her? Some backwoods bumpkin who couldn't handle his big-deal lifestyle?

"Damn it, that's not fair." Her anger heated, and yes,

her own pain stirred that heat to a boil. She jabbed a finger at his chest. "I offered to move."

He shook his head dismissively. "You wanted to move to a Vista del Mar clone and when I insisted on L.A., you made up some bull about my hormones talking. I'm not rewriting history. I remember well how you walked away from me."

Sure, she hadn't wanted to go to L.A. But she'd made the scariest offer of her life offering to leave this town and he brushed it aside as nothing? "Keep telling yourself this is all my fault if it makes you feel better." Hurt and anger and disillusionment pushed her closer to the edge. "Even when you came back two years later, you didn't have the guts to face me, to face what we feel for each other."

"And what do you feel, Sarah? Because the way I recall it, I'm the one who keeps proposing and you're the one who keeps shutting me down."

She flinched, but she wouldn't back off. "And still you don't use the word *love*. I think you're the one who's afraid to put it all on the line for fear you'll get hurt again, like when you lost your mother."

He winced and a stab of sympathy echoed through her. She tried to reach out again.

"Believe me, Rafe, I know what it's like to lose someone you love…I lost you." She touched the mantel lightly beside her silver-framed wedding photo, a part of her past that Rafe needed to accept. "I lost Quentin. I lost three babies. Taking a chance on getting my heart broken is a helluva lot scarier than anything, even leaving the only home I've known. You need to come to peace with the past. You need to let go of this grief and rage."

His eyes slid from the photo to her, his face completely devoid of emotion. "And if I don't do things the way you want?"

Hope withered inside her at his stark words. But she wasn't an eighteen-year-old girl afraid to leave home anymore.

She was a woman, confident in her own worth and unwilling to settle, even if turning him away broke her heart. "Then while I feel sorry for you, I can't be with you. You need to move on or you're going to destroy more than just Worth Industries. You're going to destroy yourself."

"I don't cave in to ultimatums anymore."

His final jab found its mark, making her realize they were truly finished. Their high school romance was over. There was no second chance for them. "You should just leave now. There's nothing left for us."

He stayed in the middle of her living room unmoving for so long she thought he might not go after all. Then he nodded curtly. "Activate the security code behind me."

Damn him for leaving and for making sure she would think of him every time she walked in and out the door with that blasted, thoughtful alarm system. She wrapped her arms around herself, already aching for him before the door closed.

Eleven

Rafe downshifted his Porsche around the corner toward a row of inexpensive condos. Bob and Penny lived in L.A. now, but he had rented a small place for them in Vista del Mar while he was in town. He'd wanted to treat them to something more elaborate. But his father—Bob—was a prideful man. Rafe only managed to wear him down to accept even this much by convincing Bob the gift would be good for Penny.

He just wished there had been someone there to help when Hannah had needed it.

Why couldn't Sarah see he was trying to make things right for his mother's memory? Ronald Worth's revelation only made things more complicated. How could the old bastard think that blood ties he'd never bothered to acknowledge would be enough to cancel out vengeance that had built over years?

He might share DNA with Ronald, but Bob was his father. And Bob was the one wrongly hurt most by Ronald and Donna Worth's machinations. Damn straight he needed to talk to Bob. He couldn't do anything about how screwed up things turned out with Sarah—God, he regretted how he'd talked to her, how it had ended—but maybe he could make some sense of his life here.

He turned off the engine in front of the two-bedroom condo a block and a half off the beach. From the street, he could see Bob on the rooftop patio, illuminated by a couple of tiki torches to keep the bugs away. Up there offered the only place in the condo with a beach view. Prideful man. Rafe wanted to believe he'd gotten honor and strength from Bob.

Just thinking of Ronald Worth's blood coursing through his veins made him want to shout his rage over the ocean. The only thing that had kept him from strangling the guy was the fact that Hannah must have seen something in him.

He *needed* to talk to Bob. His dad was his last hope to tell him he wasn't losing his mind.

The front door of the condo opened to reveal Penny in a housecoat, smiling and waving him inside. "Your dad will be so glad you stopped by."

"It's late. I apologize." For a lot of things. He'd been tough on Penny back in the beginning, finding it difficult to accept anyone would step in his mother's place.

"Nothing to apologize for. Go on up."

"Thanks, Penny." He leaned to brush a light kiss on his stepmother's cheek.

She blinked in surprise, but quickly recovered. Smiling, she patted his shoulder.

Rafe climbed both flights of stairs wrapping around and leading to the roof. Bob lounged in a white plastic chair, sipping a beer as he stared out over the night sky and ocean. He waved a hand without turning. "Grab a seat and a beer, son."

He leaned to snag a longneck from the tiny ice chest. Bob wasn't a big drinker but he enjoyed a couple of brewskies at sunset every now and again. Rafe twisted the top off and pitched it in the chest. He tipped back the pale brew.

Halfway through, he thought he might be able to talk without losing his cool again. "Spoke to Ronald Worth today."

"From the look on your face, it wasn't a peaceful end to the takeover."

Rafe rolled the bottle between his palms, staring into the colored glass, and decided he might as well get straight to the point. "He claims he's my biological father."

Slowly, Bob set his empty bottle on the ground. He exhaled long and hard before asking, "How are you handling that?"

Bob didn't deny it.

It was true.

The reality sank in with a heavy thud that reverberated inside him. Rafe hadn't realized until just that second how much hope he'd held out that Bob would say the whole thing was nuts.

"How am I handling it?" He scrubbed his jaw. "For

finding out I'm the spawn of Satan? I'm doing great. Just great." He drained the rest of the beer.

Bob snagged a fresh beer and stared out over the water for so long Rafe thought their conversation might well be over for the night. Waves echoed in the distance. Salty sea breeze gave the air bite. How many evenings had he come to Bob for advice? Plenty, up until his last year in high school when the ability to lay it all out there seemed to dry up. Rafe had attributed it to Bob finding Penny. Now he wondered if maybe he'd been to blame as well, like Sarah said. Did he shut people down subconsciously? Keep the world at arm's length so he didn't have to go through the pain of losing someone special to him like his mom?

Pretty heavy stuff to consider.

Bob folded his hands over his chest, bottle still in his clasp. "You need to abandon this hatred for Ronald Worth. It's not going to do any good. God knows I don't need or want revenge. And if she were alive, your mother would be appalled by the thought. Before she died, she came to terms with the situation. She forgave Ronald."

"Well, she's a better person than I am, then. Because I'm having a tough time letting go of what he did. And for that matter, I'm not completely okay with the fact that you and Mom lied to me for my entire life."

Shifting to face Rafe, Bob set his beer aside. "People aren't perfect, son. You've painted your mother as a saint, and God knows I loved her, but she was human, too. You've got to quit expecting the world to fit into perfect black-and-white slots."

Hadn't Sarah said much the same thing to him? And

he'd all but accused her of being narrow-minded simply because she didn't see things his way. Now hearing Bob confirm what both Worth and Sarah had said, finally Rafe felt the anger collapse inside him.

"Chase had a tough time growing up without a father. It was tough on Penny, too." Bob's face creased with concern and a fierce protectiveness. "I'm glad your mother—I'm glad that you—didn't have to live that way."

"You really do love Penny." He fully realized it and accepted it for the first time, even though his father and Penny had been married for fourteen years.

And, damn, didn't that speak volumes about how hardheaded he could be?

"Every bit as much as I loved your mother. I'm a lucky man to have found that twice. I'm sorry that my meeting Penny so soon after your mother died made things difficult for you."

Difficult? He'd damn near sabotaged his relationship with his stepbrother Chase by calling his mom unforgivable names. Chase had pummeled the crap out of him for that and he'd deserved it. Rafe realized he was the one guilty of seeing the world through a narrow focus.

Thank God Bob had been there for Hannah when Worth hadn't.

He wasn't sure he could forgive Worth for all he'd done, for the lies, but maybe he could see his way clear to keeping the factory open somehow after all.

Bob continued, "I understand that everyone makes decisions they regret." He scratched along his neck, a gesture his old man did whenever stress made his throat go tight. "Back when Ronald fired us, he arranged for a business associate to offer us jobs in another town. But I gave Hannah an ultimatum. We had to make a clean break from Ronald, no accepting any help from him. Talk about regrets? If I'd chosen differently, we could have afforded better care…." His voice cracked and faded away.

"Dad, you couldn't have known what was going to happen to Mom."

His father—his real father, the man who'd brought him up, taught him about life, sacrificed for him— gripped his shoulder. "Rafe, you're at a turning point and you need to make sure you aren't haunted by regrets and bitterness for the rest of your life."

"And if I still choose to grind Ronald Worth under my heel?"

"Then that's your decision. Nothing has changed in the way I feel about you." He squeezed Rafe's shoulder before pulling his hand away. "You're my son."

"How can you say that? Can you honestly tell me it never chewed you up inside knowing I was some other man's kid? Didn't you wonder if she still loved him?"

Bob gave him the parental "I've got your number" look. "Are we talking about your mother? Or are we discussing Sarah Richards and Quentin Dobbs?"

Rafe didn't bother answering the obvious.

"You know I love Penny, right?"

"Yeah, I do. I'm glad for you." And he genuinely was, without reservation now.

"Do you doubt that I loved your mother just as deeply?"

"That thought never crossed my mind."

"You're a smart guy." He slugged him on the arm. "Think about it. Make the connection here."

"But it's not that simple in this case. Quentin gave Sarah the life she wanted, the life I couldn't. I'm not even sure I can give her what she wants now."

"Do you love her?"

He nodded, unable to hide from the truth anymore. He'd loved Sarah Richards since high school. The feeling hadn't gone away over the years. In the back of his mind he'd always been planning for this day, when he could ride back into Vista del Mar and shower her with everything she never had. He'd just forgotten along the way to ask her what she wanted. "God, yes, I love her."

"Then don't walk away again. This time, be there for her, because when a man loves someone, that's what he does. He stays by her side." Bob had been a steadfast role model for that credo. "All the rest of it— small house, big house, little town, big town—that's just window dressing. You'll figure it out along the way."

Could it be that simple? Just tell Sarah he loved her, stick by her side and trust that the rest would work itself out? Sounded like a dangerous proposition to him. He'd always been one to plan out his every move, clearly lay out a strategy for winning. Simply launching into a life with Sarah this way was like asking him to fly by the seat of his pants.

But doing nothing meant living the rest of his days as alone as he'd felt these past fourteen years, missing her every damn minute. That didn't sound like any life at all to him.

Bob shoved to his feet. "I'm an old guy now. Need

my beauty rest. You okay to drive or would you like to stay here?"

Since he'd only had the one beer, they both knew Bob wasn't referring to alcohol intake. "I'm okay. I'm just going to drive around, air my head out."

Bob clapped him on the shoulder then pulled him in for a hard hug. Rafe hugged him back. A lot of things may have sucked about his growing-up years, but Ronald Worth had been right about one thing: Rafe had been lucky to have Bob Cameron as his father.

Five minutes later, Rafe roared away in his sports car. He could have sworn the Porsche was on autopilot as it drew him to memorable spots from when he and Sarah had dated.

To her parents' home with that big fat tree that grew conveniently close to her bedroom window.

By the high school where they'd hung out in the parking lot until the last second before the bell.

Past the Vista del Mar Beach and Tennis Club, perched on a bluff that made for perfect late-night beach walks.

And finally to Busted Bluff, where they'd driven each other crazy making out and making plans. He'd proposed to her here, desperate to have her but scared as hell he wouldn't be able to take care of her....

Rafe pulled up outside the Any Day Wedding Chapel outside of San Diego, his rusty El Camino just about on Empty. But they'd made it. Sarah was nearly levitating off her seat with happiness. He tugged at his collar only to realize he'd worn a polo shirt.

Lights from the little white chapel blink, blink,

blinked, except the W was burned out. The lot was filled with about a dozen other cars parked haphazardly by people apparently as impetuous as he and Sarah. It was graduation night at a lot of high schools in the area and apparently they weren't the only ones who'd come up with this reckless idea.

Two couples charged up the stairs lined with plastic flowers; at least one of them was drunk. This wasn't what he'd planned for when he thought of marrying Sarah. And yeah, he'd thought about it, especially over the past month. Except she wasn't leaving him much choice on how this played out, and bottom line, he didn't want to lose her.

So, he was really going to do this. He was going to marry Sarah tonight.

He pulled his hand out of his pocket and held up a thin gold band—his mother's ring. His dad had given it to him a while back, said it was his to do with as he wished. That even if he needed to pawn it someday, Hannah would be cool with that. She'd only wanted the best for her son.

Rafe placed it in Sarah's palm.

"It was my mom's," he said, his throat tight.

Her hands shook and her eyes filled with tears. "It's lovely and so very special. Rafe, I don't even know what to say."

"It doesn't have a stone or anything, but I'll get you the biggest diamond set to replace it one day."

"You will not." She folded her hand over his. "This ring will stay on my finger forever."

Forever. He would have been happier if forever started when he had more than five hundred bucks saved up, not nearly enough for a decent safe place to live and reliable wheels for both of them. His mind started churning with the practical things Sarah seemed to just brush aside with that amazing smile of hers. A smile that made him do very impractical things.

"You can keep the ring, but I'm still going to add diamonds, huge ones that will make even Ronald Worth sit up and take notice."

She clapped a hand over his mouth. "Can we please not bring up Mr. Worth? Not tonight. Honestly, as long as I have you, that's all I need."

"You're so naive sometimes." The words fell out of his mouth before he could think.

"Don't be a jerk." She thumped him on the shoulder. "I refuse to let you wreck this night for me. We're going to get married, remember? We're really going to be husband and wife by morning."

His libido gave a great big throbbing shout of encouragement. He slid his hand behind her neck and brought her to him. Kissing her, taking in the familiar taste and feel of her, he could forget all the rest. Maybe if they had sex, lots and lots of sex, he could shut up the doubt demons. Sounded like a plan to him.

Sighing that kittenish sound that always drove him crazy, Sarah eased back, her hands flat on his chest.

She stared up into his eyes, her green eyes reflecting the stars overhead. "Tell me you love me. I know you think words are silly, but I need to hear them."

"I love you, Sarah," he said automatically, already angling to kiss her again, to get as close to her as he could in the confines of his car.

Her eyebrows pinched together and he realized he

must have screwed up somehow. Damn, but women were tough to figure out.

She nibbled her bottom lip. "You don't want to do this, do you?"

"Of course I want to be with you," he said, dodging her real question. "I don't want to leave you in Vista del Mar, and God, I don't want to wait another second to be with you."

"That's not the same as wanting to marry me." She studied him with a wisdom, a seriousness he hadn't seen before.

"I do want to marry you."

"Just not now," she pressed.

All the tension of the past five months built inside him, of trying to plan out his life but how dating Sarah knocked everything off-kilter. "I would be lying if I said this was an ideal setup. Why would I want to give you a tacky quickie ceremony?" His frustration, his anger at the whole damn unfair world rose with each word. "Why would I want to take my bride to a crappy one-room apartment in the worst section of town? But there aren't a lot of options here until I start making serious money."

"I'm in your way." The starlight faded from her eyes.

"Damn it, Sarah." He clasped her shoulders. "Don't put it like that."

"You don't want to get married."

He stayed silent this time.

She looked at the ring in her hand, then pressed it into his palm and folded his fingers over it. "I'll make this easier for you. We're not getting married. Go to

Los Angeles and follow your dreams. Mine are in Vista del Mar."

She leaned across the seat and pressed her lips to his, holding, not moving, her eyes squeezed shut and a single tear escaping. "I'm going to get out of the car now and I do not want you to follow me. I'm going to call my grandmother for a ride. And I mean it. I don't want to see you again. I can't. Goodbye, Rafe."

She slipped out of the car and into the wedding chapel. Relief jockeyed with regret in his gut. He didn't follow her inside, but he would wait around just out of sight to make sure her grandmother arrived safely. After that, he was leaving for Los Angeles. He had five hundred bucks saved up.

This wasn't goodbye, damn it. He would be back for her, once he made enough money to give her a safer, more secure life. She wouldn't have to wait long. Just three years, four at the most, until he could work while going to night school. He wouldn't last longer than that without her anyway.

And God forbid some other guy try to step into his place.

Because he would be back. And when he returned, he would claim Sarah as his wife....

Rafe sat in his Porsche on Busted Bluff, the past tugging at him like the waves on the beach drawing away sand from the shore. The breeze and the sound whispered in through his open windows, and suddenly he wasn't thinking about his past with Sarah. He could swear he heard his mother.

He wasn't a mystical man by any stretch, but it was

almost as if she sat there beside him, talking softly. She'd always been good about that, just carrying the conversation since he wasn't much of a chatty guy himself. She didn't push him, simply filled in the empty spaces of conversation. Her voice was lyrical even though she couldn't sing worth a damn. Her presence was soothing enough.

Near the end of her life, when she'd been so wrung out from the sickness she couldn't walk, he would carry her to the car even though he didn't have a license and drive her to the beach, oxygen tank and all. It was her favorite place. She'd talked so softly at the end, struggling for air, but she spoke even more, faster then, as if she needed to cram a lifetime of wisdom into those last weeks.

He'd worked so damn hard to make her proud. He'd funded a whole charity foundation for the disadvantaged in her honor. And suddenly, he realized she would be so very disappointed in him.

Hannah had given up everything to keep him. She'd given up everything to build a family.

And he'd tossed away his chance at a family, a chance with Sarah, a woman far more valuable than anything he'd acquired over the past fourteen years. He owed his mother better than the man he'd become. He owed Sarah.

And he intended to come through for them both this time.

The next day, Sarah plastered on the best pretend smile she could scavenge for her grandmother's big birthday bash. Her feet aching in her black satin pumps that matched her simple black sheath, she circulated to make sure all the platters were stocked, the guests happily served.

The gathering was in full swing at the Beach and Tennis Club. Ronald Worth had financed the gig as a gift to his former employee. As Kathleen Richards had lived in Vista del Mar her whole life, the guest list was long.

Party tents were set up outside, tables laden with everything from seafood to a carving station. A bubbling champagne fountain competed with the swoosh of the waves. Frothy white gauze trimmed in silver fluttered in the wind. A live swing band played off to the side with a wooden dance floor laid out under the stars.

Her grandmother was queen of the ball, dancing with Chase Larson. Her parents were kicking up their heels for once, recreation so rare for the two of them working double shifts all the time. Bob and Penny showed off a two-step with twirls and dips.

Rafe hadn't come to the party, although she hadn't expected him to attend. He didn't much care for the Tennis Club, Ronald Worth—or her—anymore.

Sarah couldn't help but think of dancing under the stars with Rafe in Nevada a short time ago. He'd obviously learned to dance from his father—Bob.

Rafe had lost his mother and now received such shocking news about his paternity as well. She ached for him and all he'd been through, even as she wanted to shake him for putting up such impenetrable walls to protect his heart.

Although right now, she wouldn't mind a little extra protection for her own emotions. She pivoted away from all the blissfully happy dance couples—and almost slammed into Juan Rodriguez plucking a leaf from a trailing fern.

Sarah forced her smile back in place. "You did a magnificent job with the floral arrangements, Mr. Rodriguez. The hydrangeas are particularly stunning."

"It was an honor to contribute to your grandmother's celebration. She is a special lady, like her granddaughter," he said gallantly.

His Zenlike quality soothed her frazzled nerves and it was nice not to stand alone feeling miserable for a change.

"Thank you, that's kind." Sarah searched for a way to extend the conversation. "I'm still not having much luck growing bougainvillea in my backyard. Do you have any more advice?"

"Actually—" he plucked a glass of champagne from a passing waiter's tray "—the best person I know to look to for advice about bougainvillea is Rafe."

She couldn't have heard him right. Was the man losing his edge with the passing years? "Rafe Cameron?"

"None other. He was the best helper I ever employed." He sipped his drink, eying her intuitively over the crystal flute.

"Employed?" But Rafe had worked construction after school. "I didn't know he worked for you."

"The last semester of his senior year, he came to the Worth greenhouse every morning before school to earn extra money—" smiling, he winked "—and pick up some exotic flowers for the special lady in his life."

And she'd never known. She'd wondered how he afforded all of those flowers he'd showered on her while they'd been dating, had even carried that piece of their romance with her all these years in nurturing her garden. Now, after fourteen years, the mystery of how he'd managed to give her so many flowers was finally solved.

Not only had he worked himself into the ground for her, but he'd swallowed his pride to take a job on the Worth estate. That had to have galled him, yet he'd done it—for her. Tears stung her eyes. Why hadn't he told her?

More importantly, why hadn't she thought to ask?

Realization prickled over her, stinging and not at all comfortable as she realized her own shortcomings. She'd never really pushed Rafe for answers on anything, just plowing ahead with her own assumptions. She'd let fear drive her then, just as she was doing now. After only a handful of days with Rafe, she'd bailed right when things got complicated.

Yes, she'd loved Quentin and the quiet life they'd built together. But they'd never challenged each other. They'd played it safe. With Rafe, that wasn't an option. They were opinionated and their emotions were messy. And it was time for her to grow up and accept the challenge, the risk, the lifelong adventure of loving Rafe Cameron.

If it wasn't too late.

As if conjured from her thoughts, he stepped through the French doors leading from the club to the outdoor party area. He looked every bit as handsome in his tuxedo now as he had at their high school prom. Back then, others had worn colorful cummerbunds and ties, but Rafe had kept it basic. His presence commanded a room all on its own.

Smoothing her damp palms down her simple, fitted black dress, she winged a grateful prayer for Time Again's evening-gown selection. She checked her hair, swept up with tiny flowers woven in. She gathered her nerve to march right up to him, only to realize Rafe was already walking toward her.

As he parted the crowd, he didn't so much as pause for all the greetings and questions, simply nodding a hello. He even gave a tight nod to Ronald Worth.

Could she be reading a hopeful message into such a simple gesture because she wanted it to be true so very badly? Regardless, she would stand by Rafe this time, even as she stood up to him. And through it all she wouldn't lose sight of the boy who'd worked overtime to give her flowers. The man who'd built her dream house.

Her lover who stood in front of her with his hand extended.

"If you're going to dump a pitcher of tea in my lap, Kitten, let's get that part out of the way first."

Her smile turned real for the first time since he'd walked out of her door. "Your tuxedo is safe."

"Good, now would you like to dance?" He linked his fingers with hers, lifting her hand lightly. "We need to talk and things always seem easier for us when we're touching."

His words, the feel of his skin against hers raised goose bumps of awareness. She closed her hand around his and he pulled her into his arms, against his chest.

Curious eyes watched them, but she didn't care one whit. Rafe had come back for her. And this time, she wasn't going to push him away without giving him a fair chance.

His mouth grazed her temple, his breath warm against her ear as he said softly, "I've never been the chatty, poetic type. I'm more about making my point and moving forward."

"And that point would be?" Her head spun from the feel of him against her as much as the intricate steps whirling her around the dance floor.

"Right now, I would like to find those words, because you're too important to let go." His hold on her strengthened, as if instinctively wanting to keep her near. "I was an idiot fourteen years ago. Once I cooled down after our fight outside the wedding chapel, I should have come right back to you."

She'd been thinking how she hadn't given him a real chance and now he was thinking the same? They'd both been so young. Sarah angled back to look in his cerulean eyes that had mesmerized her since she was a teenager. "Then you wouldn't have everything you've built with Cameron Enterprises."

"I wonder now if maybe I would have had it all sooner with you by my side." His voice went hoarse with intensity. "Sarah, I'm a better man, make better decisions, see new possibilities, when I'm with you."

Her pulse sped, love swelling inside her with every unexpected declaration from his mouth. "That's really a beautiful thing to say."

"I don't know if you can forgive me. I'm not sure if I deserve forgiving for letting you down." He brought their clasped hands to his chest, right over the steady beat of his heart. "But I'm going to try my damnedest to win you back anyway. I don't want to throw away what we have again."

She opened her mouth to tell him how much she loved him, how sorry she was as well, but he placed a finger over her lips.

"Shh... I need to say some things first." He danced her to the far end of the floor then onto the sand, away from the crowd. "I've been thinking about the factory. Maybe it doesn't need to be closed. I can't keep things as is, but an upgrade of some sort could be in order."

She couldn't believe her ears. He wasn't just saying he wanted to win her back. He was showing her his commitment to making a change as well. "Like what?"

"I haven't gotten that far yet, but I look forward to figuring it out. I'm going to put together a focus group from the employee staff working with my Dream Team. I have faith we'll come up with an option to save jobs, hopefully create more. I'm not ready to give up on Vista del Mar."

His feet slowed until they stopped dancing and he simply held her under the stars and moon as he'd done so many times before. "I'm not ever going to be ready to give up on us."

He dropped to one knee in the sand along the Vista del Mar shore. He dipped his hand in his pocket and pulled out a simple gold band she recognized well from their near-elopement fourteen years ago.

"Sarah Richards, I have loved you since we were in high school, and I love you even more today. Will you do me the immense honor of letting me love you for the rest of my life by becoming my bride?"

Her heart squeezed tight with excitement, with possibility and most of all, with love. She dropped to her knees in front of him and threw her arms around his neck. "Yes, a million times yes, I will marry you and I look forward to showing you every single day just how much I love you, whether we live here or anywhere else in the world, as long as we're together."

He slid the ring on her finger, sealing it with a kiss as the partiers up on the bluff applauded. Sarah closed her fingers, holding the precious gift in place. She knew the ceremony was just a formality.

Because here, tonight, she had claimed her small-town husband.

Epilogue

Three months later

On the edge of the dock, Rafe stood holding hands with Sarah looking over their new beachfront home. He'd sold the condo in lieu of a real house. The two-story yellow stucco wasn't as large as he'd originally wanted to give her, but he had to confess, Sarah's choice was a helluva lot more tasteful than the mammoth monstrosity he'd suggested when the Realtor showed them properties. He was working on a little less conspicuous consumption, a lot more embracing home life with Sarah.

Their housewarming party was well underway, the last of the guests having arrived. The festivities were being held outside under the warm Pacific sun since they hadn't decorated the inside yet. But they had a lifetime to do that. Starting today.

Now he and Sarah could move on to the real reason for the gathering. He brought Sarah's hand up to his mouth, kissing the engagement ring he'd bought her. He looked forward to placing his mother's wedding band on her finger before the sun set.

They'd organized a small surprise marriage ceremony with just their family and friends in attendance. Originally, they'd intended to get married next year in a huge service, but after a summer of dates—lunches, dinners, long weekends spent in bed or on the beach making love, talking, then making love again—they'd both decided they'd waited long enough. They didn't want the stress and mayhem of planning a huge wedding. Flowers from Mr. Rodriguez lined the dock as well as the cabana on the beach where the reception would be held.

They were ready to be husband and wife.

Squeezing Sarah's hands in his, Rafe nodded for the music to begin.

A simple guitar tune filled the air as the famous rock balladeer Ward Miller sang with his bride Ana looking on.

There were certainly plenty of witnesses on hand for the occasion, even by just inviting those close to them. Along with Sarah's parents and grandmother, Ronald Worth stood with his daughter. Emma cradled her infant son in her arms as she leaned back against Chase. Rafe wasn't ready to have family picnics with Worth by any means, but he'd gotten past wanting to pound the guy. Peace and acceptance were working their way through his system thanks to Sarah's influence. His half brother, Brandon, stood with his new wife, Paige, a baby on the way. And they weren't the only ones expecting. William and Margaret Tanner had announced their big news as well.

Rafe looked forward to the day he and Sarah adopted a child. Even if by some miracle they conceived, he felt drawn to adoption, to live out his father's—Bob's—legacy. Blood relationships didn't always dictate bonds.

There, on the beach and along the dock, they were surrounded by examples of long-term happiness—Bob and Penny. Sarah's parents. Mr. and Mrs. Rodriguez. Max Preston stood with his wife and son. And mingled in with it all, Rafe could swear he heard his mother's blessing whispered on the ocean breeze twining around all of them, a unified town.

Flowers and happiness seemed to bloom all around them. With pots of young bougainvillea lining the dock and the profusion of fresh flowers in Sarah's bouquet, he was grinning at the way his soon-to-be wife coaxed beauty all around her. After a third friend asked her for tips on landscaping last month, Sarah had gotten the idea to go into business with Juan Rodriguez, bringing their different touches in the garden to other homes around Vista del Mar. Rafe couldn't wait to offer her a fat contract to spruce up the grounds surrounding the factory. He was all about going green after the unhealthy atmosphere that had dogged the place in the past. But for now, he'd settled on passing her some start-up funds. He owed Juan Rodriguez more than he could repay for that job in high school, for all the flowers for Sarah.

Even the factory issue had come to a happy conclusion once the right opportunity came out of his focus group. He'd temporarily halted operations at the plant so it could be converted to a high-tech facility for advanced microchips. It would benefit both the town and Cameron Enterprises in the long term. Rafe had drawn up offers for all his workers with a competitive benefits package, and pay for higher education, if the workers wanted to go back to school. His headquarters for Cameron Enterprises were located here now, and he wanted his employees to be happy.

Hannah's Hope had taught him a lot about reaching and giving back. Next month, in fact, the organization would be featured in *Newsweek* as a model of revitalization that had given their small American town a second life.

And through it all, he'd found a second chance at life with Sarah.

The preacher took his place at the head of the dock as the love song's final notes faded out over the ocean. Rafe faced Sarah, so gorgeous in her white flowy dress, flowers in her auburn hair, her feet bare.

He'd chosen a simple tan suit, no pomp and circumstance. Today was about starting the rest of his life off on the right foot, his priorities in place.

With Sarah. His first love. And at last, his wife.

* * * * *

Harlequin® Desire

COMING NEXT MONTH

Available July 12, 2011

#2095 CAUGHT IN THE BILLIONAIRE'S EMBRACE
Elizabeth Bevarly

#2096 ONE NIGHT, TWO HEIRS
Maureen Child
Texas Cattleman's Club: The Showdown

#2097 THE TYCOON'S TEMPORARY BABY
Emily McKay
Billionaires and Babies

#2098 A LONE STAR LOVE AFFAIR
Sara Orwig
Stetsons & CEOs

#2099 ONE MONTH WITH THE MAGNATE
Michelle Celmer
Black Gold Billionaires

#2100 FALLING FOR THE PRINCESS
Sandra Hyatt

You can find more information on upcoming
Harlequin® titles, free excerpts and more at
www.HarlequinInsideRomance.com.

USA TODAY *bestselling author B.J. Daniels
takes you on a trip to Whitehorse, Montana,
and the Chisholm Cattle Company.*

RUSTLED

Available July 2011 from Harlequin Intrigue.

As the dust settled, Dawson got his first good look at the rustler. A pair of big Montana sky-blue eyes glared up at him from a face framed by blond curls.

A woman rustler?

"You have to let me go," she hollered as the roar of the stampeding cattle died off in the distance.

"So you can finish stealing my cattle? I don't think so." Dawson jerked the woman to her feet.

She reached for the gun strapped to her hip hidden under her long barn jacket.

He grabbed the weapon before she could, his eyes narrowing as he assessed her. "How many others are there?" he demanded, grabbing a fistful of her jacket. "I think you'd better start talking before I tear into you."

She tried to fight him off, but he was on to her tricks and pinned her to the ground. He was suddenly aware of the soft curves beneath the jean jacket she wore under her coat.

"You have to listen to me." She ground out the words from between her gritted teeth. "You have to let me go. If you don't they will come back for me and they will kill you. There are too many of them for you to fight off alone. You won't stand a chance and I don't want your blood on my hands."

"I'm touched by your concern for me. Especially after you just tried to pull a gun on me."

"I wasn't going to shoot you."

Dawson hauled her to her feet and walked her the rest of the way to his horse. Reaching into his saddlebag, he pulled out a length of rope.

"You can't tie me up."

He pulled her hands behind her back and began to tie her wrists together.

"If you let me go, I can keep them from coming back," she said. "You have my word." She let out an unladylike curse. "I'm just trying to save your sorry neck."

"And I'm just going after my cattle."

"Don't you mean your boss's cattle?"

"Those cattle are mine."

"*You're* a Chisholm?"

"Dawson Chisholm. And you are…?"

"Everyone calls me Jinx."

He chuckled. "I can see why."

Bronco busting, falling in love…it's all in a day's work.
Look for the rest of their story in

RUSTLED

Available July 2011 from Harlequin Intrigue
wherever books are sold.